M000297656

GRAZIA DELEDDA

The Mother
(La madre)

a Novel

translated by Mary G. Steegman

In cobertina: particulare de su pintadu de James Abbott McNeill Whistler "*Whistler's Mother*", 1871, ògiu a pitzu de tela, 144,3 × 162,4 cm.

First published in 1922 by Jonathan Cape, London, *The Woman & the Priest* was translated from the Italian by Mary G. Steegmann. In november 1923 The Macmillan Company of New York published it with the title *The Mother* and a note and foreword by the translator. A second edition was published in 1928 by Jonathan Cape with an introduction by David Herbert Lawrence.

Drafting and revision of texts by Francesco Cheratzu.

Colletzione "Le Grazie"

PoD Edition

Second edition

Original title: *La madre* (Treves, 1920).
Translated from the Italian by Mary G. Steegmann.

Grazia Deledda
The Mother
ISBN **978-88-3309-040-5**

Editziones NOR, carrera Lombardia 11, I-09074 Ilartzi (Aristanis), Sardigna.
www.nor-web.eu – info@nor-web.eu

PREFACE[1]

Novelists who have laid the scenes of their stories almost invariably in one certain country or district, or amongst one certain class of people, or who have dealt with one special topic or interest, are apt to be called monotonous by a public which merely reads to kill time or is always craving for new sensations in its literature. But to another and more serious class of reader this very fidelity to scene and steadfastness of outlook is one of the principal incentives to take up each fresh work of such writers, for it is safe to assume that they are writing about what they really know and understand and their work may be expected to deepen and develop with each succeeding book.

Amongst such writers Grazia Deledda takes high rank. One of the foremost women novelists of Italy, if not the very first, she has been writing for some five and twenty years, and though almost always utilizing the same setting for her novels, each succeeding one has shown a different leading idea, a new variation upon the eternal theme of more or less primitive human nature.

Madame Deledda is a Sardinian by birth and parentage. She was born at Nuoro, the little inland town that figures so often in her books, and there she spent her first youth amongst the shepherds and peasants and small landed proprietors such as live again in her pages. On her marriage to a young Lombard she left

---

1) Preface to the 1923 edition by The Macmillan Company, New York. The translator's note of the 1922 London edition was also included but the title changed:
«*The Mother** (*The Woman and the Priest**) is an unusual book, both in its story and its setting in a remote Sardinian hill village, half civilized and superstitious. But the chief interest lies in the psychological study of the two chief characters, and the action of the story takes place so rapidly (all within the space of two days) and the actual drama is so interwoven with the mental conflict, and all so forced by circumstances, that it is almost Greek in its simple and inevitable tragedy.

The book is written without offence to any creed or opinions, and touches on no questions of either doctrine or Church government. It is just a human problem, the result of primitive human nature against man-made laws it cannot understand.
* Translated from the Italian novel *La madre*».

Sardinia and went with her husband to Rome, where she still lives and works, with the steadfast aim of yet further perfecting herself in her art.

As may be expected, the action of her numerous novels takes place principally in her native island of Sardinia, with its wild and rugged background of mountain, rock, and wide tracts of thicket and shrub. The people of Sardinia, chiefly shepherds, agriculturists, and fishermen, differ considerably from those of the mainland, and a graver and less vivacious demeanour than most other Italians, a strict sense of honour, and hospitality regarded as an actual duty, makes them more resemble the ancient Spanish race with which indeed they are probably distantly akin.

The life of the poorer islanders is usually one of great privation, and ceaseless hard work is required to win a subsistence from the soil in the mountain uplands, exposed alternately to the scorching summer sun and the fierce gales and icy winds of winter. The native dress is still worn, though the fashion is dying out, and the old traditional superstitions and half pagan beliefs in witchcraft and the evil eye survive side by side with a profound and simple religious faith, a combination only possible in the islands, as in the remoter parts of the mainland, where the people never go far from their native districts and seldom come in contact with outside influences.

Nowhere, perhaps, has Grazia Deledda better portrayed this mingling of inbred superstition with Church-directed religion than in *The Mother*. Here the scene is laid in the remote and only half civilized hill village of Aar, and while the action of the story is dramatic and swift (it takes place all within the space of two days), the chief interest lies in the psychological study of the two principal characters, and the actual drama is so interwoven with the mental conflict, so developed by outward circumstances, that it is almost Greek in its simple and inevitable tragedy.

We meet here many of the inhabitants of the mountain district; the old hunter who has turned solitary through dread of men, the domineering keeper and his dog, the wholly delightful boy sacristan and his friends. But the figures in whom the interest centres are, first and foremost, the mother of the young parish priest of Aar (hence the title *La Madre* in the original Italian), Paul, the priest himself, and Agnes, the lonely woman who wrecks the lives of both mother and son.

The love story of Paul is doubtless common enough. As is generally the case, especially with priests promoted from the humbler ranks of life, he made his vows whilst still too young to understand all that he was professing and renouncing. He had been taught that divine love was all-sufficing, to the exclusion of any other kind, and when human love overtook him he was too inexperienced and too weak to have any chance in the struggle for victory – and he desperately trusted to the hazard of events to save him when his own self-deception and cowardice had failed – when confronted with the greater strength and moral honesty of the woman.

It is the fine and consistently drawn character of Maria Maddalena, however, that claims the reader's whole sympathy. Poor, ignorant, able neither to read nor write, she has brought up her boy by her own hard work and has achieved the peasant's ambition of seeing him admitted to the priesthood and given charge of a parish. For a time all goes well, until the inevitable woman appears on the scene, and then suddenly she finds her son gone beyond her reach and exposed to perils she dare not contemplate. In her unquestioning acceptance of the Church's laws her simple mind is only filled with terror lest Paul should break those laws. But while she is inexorable with the priest her heart yearns over the young man, tender with his grief, and, spurred on by a phantom, a dream, her love and her intelligence begin for the first time to regret the natural happiness he is denied and to question the Church's right to impose such a denial. And at last the struggle and the suspense grow more than she can bear and live.

It should be stated emphatically that the book is written without the least offence to any creed or opinion whatsoever, and touches on no question of either doctrine or Church government. It is just a human problem, the revolt of primitive human nature in distress against man-made laws it suffers from and cannot understand.

Mary G. Steegman

INTRODUCTION

Grazia Deledda is already one of the elder living writers of Italy, and though her work does not take on quite so rapidly as the novels of Fogazzaro, or even D'Annunzio, that peculiarly obscuring nebulousness of the past-which-is-only-just-gone-by, still, the dimness has touched it. It is curious that fifteen or twenty years ago should seem so much more remote than fifty or eighty years ago. But perhaps it is organically necessary to us that our feelings should die, temporarily, towards that strange intermediate period which lies between present actuality and the revived past. We can hardly bear to recall the emotions of twenty or fifteen years ago, hardly at all, whereas we respond again quite vividly to the emotions of Jane Austen or Dickens, nearer a hundred years ago. There, the past is safely and finally past. The past of fifteen years ago is till yeastily working in us.

It takes a really good writer to make us overcome our repugnance to the just-gone-by emotions. Even D'Annunzio's novels are hardly readable at present: Matilde Serao's still less so. But we can still read Grazia Deledda, with genuine interest.

The reason is that, though she is not a first-class genius, she belongs to more than just her own day. She does more than reproduce the temporarily psychological condition of her period. She has a background, and she deals with something more fundamental than sophisticated feeling. She does not penetrate, as a great genius does, the very sources of human passion and motive. She stays far short of that. But what she does do is to create the passionate complex of primitive populace.

To do this, one must have an isolated populace: just as Thomas Hardy isolates Wessex. Grazia Deledda has an isolated island to herself, her own island of Sardinia, that she loves so deeply: especially the more northerly, mountainous part of Sardinia.

2) From Grazia Deledda, *The Mother*, with an Introduction by David Herbert Lawrence; London: Jonathan Cape, 1928.

Still Sardinia is one of the wildest, remotest part of Europe, with a strange people and a mysterious past of its own. There is still an old mystery in the air, over the forest slopes of Mount Gennargentu, as there is over some old Druid places, the mystery of an unevolved people. The war, of course, partly gutted Sardinia, as it gutted everywhere. But the island is still a good deal off the map, on the face of the earth.

An island of rigid conventions, the rigid conventions of barbarism, and at the same time, the fierce violence of the instinctive passions. A savage tradition of chastity, with a savage lust of the flesh. A barbaric overlordship of the gentry, with a fierce indomitableness of the servile classes. A lack of public opinion, a lack of belonging to any other part of the world, a lack of mental awakening, which makes inland Sardinia almost as savage as Benin, and makes Sardinian singing as wonderful and almost as wild as any on earth. It is the human instinct still uncontaminated. The money-sway still did not govern central Sardinia, in the days of Grazia Deledda's books, twenty, a dozen years ago, before the war. Instead there was a savage kind of aristocracy and feudalism, and a rule of ancient instinct, instinct with the definite but indescribable tang of the aboriginal people of the island, not absorbed into the world: instinct often at war with the Italian government; a determined savage individualism often breaking with the law, or driven into brigandage: but human, of the great human mystery.

It is this old Sardinia, at least being brought to heel, which is the real theme of Grazia Deledda's books. She is fascinated by her island and its folks, more than by the problems of the human psyche. And therefore this book, *The Mother*, is perhaps one of the least typical of her novels, one of the most "continental". Because here, she has a definite universal theme: the consecrated priest and the woman. But she keeps on forgetting her theme. She becomes more interested in the death of the old hunter, in the doings of the boy Antiochus, in the exorcising of the spirit of the little girl possessed. She is herself somewhat bored by the priest's hesitations; she shows herself suddenly impatient, a pagan sceptical of the virtues of chastity, even in consecrated priests; she is touched, yet annoyed by the pathetic, tiresome old mother who made her son a priest out of ambition, and who simply expires in the terror of a public exposure: and, in short, she makes a bit of a mess of the book, because she started a problem she didn't quite dare to solve. She shirks the issue atrociously. But neither will the modern spirit solve the problem by killing off the fierce instincts that made the problem. As for Grazia Deledda, first she started by sympathising with the mother, and then must sympathise savagely with the young woman, and then can't make up her mind. She kills off the old mother in disgust at the old woman's triumph, so leaving the priest and the young woman hanging in space. As a sort of problem-story, it is disappointing. No doubt, if the priest had gone off with the woman, as he first intended, then all the authoress' sympathy would have fallen to the abandoned old mother. As it is, the sympathy falls between two stools, and the title *La Madre* is not really justified. The mother turns out not to be the heroine.

But the interest of this book lies, not in plot or characterisation, but in the representation of sheer instinctive life. The love of the priest for the woman is sheer instinctive passion, pure and undefiled by sentiment. As such it is worthy of respect, for in other books on this theme the instinct is swamped and extinguished in sentiment. Here, however, the instinct of direct sex is so strong and so vivid, that only the other blind instinct of mother-obedience, the child-instinct, can overcome it. All the priest's education and Christianity are really mere snuff of the candle. The old, wild instinct of a mother's ambition for her son defeats the other wild instinct of sexual mating. An old woman who has never had any sex life – and it is astonishing, in barbaric half-civilisations, how many people are denied a sex life; she succeeds, by her old barbaric maternal power over her son, in finally killing his sex life too. It is the suicide of semi-barbaric natures under the sway of a dimly-comprehended Christianity, and falsely conceived ambition.

The old, blind life of instinct, and chiefly frustrated instinct and the rage thereof, as it is seen in the Sardinian hinterland, this is Grazia Deledda's absorption. The desire of the boy Antiochus to be a priest is an instinct: perhaps an instinctive recoil from his mother's grim priapism. The dying man escapes from the village, back to the rocks, instinctively needing to die in the wilds. The feeling of Agnes, the woman who loves the priest, is sheer female instinctive passion, something as in Emily Bronte. It too has the ferocity of the frustrated instinct, and is bare and stark, lacking any of the graces of sentiment. This saves it from "dating" as D'Annunzio's passions date. Sardinia is by no means a land for Romeos and Juliets, nor even Virgins of the Rocks. It is rather a land of Wuthering Heights.

The book, of course, loses a good deal in translation, as is inevitable. In the mouth of the simple people, Italian is a purely instinctive language, with the rhythm of the instinctive rather than the mental processes. There are also many instinct-words with meanings never clearly mentally defined. In fact, nothing is brought to real mental clearness, everything goes by in a stream of more or less vague, more or less realised feeling, with a natural midst or glow of sensation over everything, that counts more than the actual words said; and which, alas, it is almost impossible to reproduce in the more cut-and-dried northern languages, where every word has its fixed value and meaning like so much coinage. A language can be killed by over-precision, killed especially as an effective medium for the conveyance of instinctive passion and instinctive emotion. One feels this, reading a translation from the Italian. And though Grazia Deledda is not masterly as Giovanni Verga is, yet, in Italian at least, she can put us into the mood and rhythm of Sardinia like a true artist, an artist whose work is sound and enduring.

D.H. Lawrence

THE MOTHER[3]

Tonight again Paul was preparing to go out, it seemed. From her room adjoining his the mother could hear him moving about furtively, perhaps waiting to go out until she should have extinguished her light and got into bed.

She put out her light, but she did not get into bed.

Seated close against the door, she clasped her hands tightly together, those work-worn hands of a servant, pressing the thumbs one upon the other to give herself courage; but every moment her uneasiness increased and overcame her obstinate hope that her son would sit down quietly, as he used to do, and begin to read, or else go to bed. For a few minutes, indeed, the young priest's cautious steps were silent. She felt herself all alone. Outside, the noise of the wind mingled with the murmuring of the trees which grew on the ridge of high ground behind the little presbytery; not a high wind, but incessant, monotonous, that sounded as though it were enveloping the house in some creaking, invisible band, ever closer and closer, trying to uproot it from its foundations and drag it to the ground.

The mother had already closed the house door and barricaded it with two crossed bars, in order to prevent the devil, who on windy nights roams abroad in search of souls, from penetrating into the house. As a matter of fact, however, she put little faith in such things. And now she reflected with bitterness, and a vague contempt of herself, that the evil spirit was already inside the little presbytery, that it drank from her Paul's cup and hovered about the mirror he had hung on the wall near his window.

Just then she heard Paul moving about again. Perhaps he was actually standing in front of the mirror, although that was forbid-

3) In the first English edition (*The Woman & the Priest*) a chapter arrangement was introduced that was not present in the original Italian version. We have reverted back to the former structure since it seems – in our opinion – to better convey the drama and dynamism of the plot which evolves in an extremely short time period: less than three days (Editor's note).

den to priests. But what had Paul not allowed himself for some considerable time now?

The mother remembered that lately she had several times come upon him gazing at himself in the glass like any woman, cleaning and polishing his nails, or brushing his hair, which he had left to grow long and then turned back over his head, as though trying to conceal the holy mark of the tonsure. And then he made use of perfumes, he brushed his teeth with scented powder, and even combed out his eyebrows.

She seemed to see him now as plainly as though the dividing wall did not exist, a black figure against the white background of his room; a tall, thin figure, almost too tall, going to and fro with the heedless steps of a boy, often stumbling and slipping about, but always holding himself erect. His head was a little too large for the thin neck, his face pale and overshadowed by the prominent forehead that seemed to force the brows to frown and the long eyes to droop with the burden of it. But the powerful jaw, the wide, full mouth and the resolute chin seemed in their turn to revolt with scorn against this oppression, yet not be able to throw it off.

But now he halted before the mirror and his whole face lighted up, the eyelids opened to the full and the pupils of his clear brown eyes shone like diamonds.

Actually, in the depths of her maternal heart, his mother delighted to see him so handsome and strong, and then the sound of his furtive steps moving about again recalled her sharply to her anxiety.

He was going out, there could be no more doubt about that. He opened the door of his room and stood still again. Perhaps he, too, was listening to the sounds without, but there was nothing to be heard save the encircling wind beating ever against the house.

The mother made an effort to rise from her chair, to cry out "My son, Paul, child of God, stay here!" but a power stronger than her own will kept her down. Her knees trembled as though trying to rebel against that infernal power; her knees trembled, but her feet refused to move, and it was as though two compelling hands were holding her down upon her seat.

Thus Paul could steal noiselessly downstairs, open the door and go out, and the wind seemed to engulf him and bear him away in a flash.

Only then was she able to rise and light her lamp again. But even this was only achieved with difficulty, because, instead of igniting, the matches left long violet streaks on the wall wherever she struck them. But at last the little brass lamp threw a dim radiance over the small room, bare and poor as that of a servant, and she opened the door and stood there, listening. She was still trembling, yet she moved stiffly and woodenly, and with her large head and her short, broad figure clothed in rusty black she looked as though she had been hewn with an axe, all of a piece, from the trunk of an oak.

From her threshold she looked down the slate stairs descending steeply between whitewashed walls, at the bottom of which the door shook upon its hinges with the violence of the wind. And when she saw the two bars which Paul had unfastened and left leaning against the wall she was filled with sudden wild anger.

Ah no, she must defeat the devil. Then she placed her light on the floor at the top of the stairs, descended and went out, too.

The wind seized hold of her roughly, blowing out her skirts and the handkerchief over her head, as though it were trying to force her back into the house. But she knotted the handkerchief tightly under her chin and pressed forward with bent head, as though butting aside all obstacles in her path. She felt her way past the front of the presbytery, along the wall of the kitchen garden and past the front of the church, but at the corner of the church she paused. Paul had turned there, and swiftly, like some great black bird, his cloak flapping round him, he had almost flown across the field that extended in front of an old house built close against the ridge of land that shut in the horizon above the village.

The uncertain light, now blue, now yellow, as the moon's face shone clear or was traversed by big clouds, illumined the long grass of the field, the little raised *piazza*, in front of the church and presbytery, and the two lines of cottages on either side of the steep road, which wound on and downwards till it lost itself amidst the trees in the valley. And in the centre of the valley, like another grey and winding road, was the river that flowed on and in its turn lost itself amidst the rivers and roads of the fantastic landscape that the wind-driven clouds alternately revealed and concealed on that distant horizon that lay beyond the valley's edge.

In the village itself not a light was to be seen, nor even a thread of smoke. They were all asleep by now in the poverty-stricken cottages, which clung to the grassy hill-side like two rows of sheep, whilst the church with its slender tower, itself protected by the ridge of land behind it, might well represent the shepherd leaning upon his staff.

The elder trees which grew along the parapet of the piazza before the church were bending and tossing furiously in the wind, black and shapeless monsters in the gloom, and in answer to their rustling cry came the lament of the poplars and reeds in the valley. And in all this dolour of the night, the moaning wind and the moon drowning midst the angry clouds, was merged the sorrow of the mother seeking for her son.

Until that moment she had tried to deceive herself with the hope that she would see him going before her down into the village to visit some sick parishioner, but instead, she beheld him running as though spurred on by the devil towards the old house under the ridge.

And in that old house under the ridge there was no one save a woman, young, healthy and alone...

Instead of approaching the principal entrance like an ordinary visitor, he went straight to the little door in the orchard wall, and immediately it opened and closed again behind him like a black mouth that had swallowed him up.

Then she too ran across the meadow, treading in the path his feet had made in the long grass; straight to the little door she ran, and she put her open hands against it, pushing with all her strength. But the little door remained closed, it even seemed to repulse her by an active power of its own, and the woman felt she must strike it and cry aloud. She looked at the wall and touched it as though to test its solidity, and at last in despair she bent her head and listened intently. But nothing could be heard save the creaking and rustling of the trees inside the orchard, friends and accomplices of their mistress, trying to cover with their own noises all other sounds there within.

But the mother would not be beaten, she must hear and know – or rather – since in her inmost soul she already knew the truth, she wanted some excuse for still deceiving herself.

Careless now whether she were seen or not, she walked the whole length of the orchard wall, past the front of the house, and beyond it as far as the big gate of the courtyard; and as she went she touched the stones as though seeking one that would give way and leave a hole whereby she might enter in. But everything was solid, compact, fast shut – the big entrance gate, the hall door, the barred windows – like the openings in a fortress.

At that moment the moon emerged from behind the clouds and shone out clear in a lake of blue, illuminating the reddish frontage of the house, which was partly overshadowed by the deep eaves of the overhanging grass-grown roof; the inside shutters of the windows were closed and the panes of glass shone like greenish mirrors, reflecting the drifting clouds and the patches of blue sky and the tossing branches of the trees upon the ridge.

Then she turned back, striking her head against the iron rings let into the wall for tethering horses. Again she halted in front of the chief entrance, and before that big door with its three granite steps, its Gothic porch and iron gate, she felt suddenly humiliated, powerless to succeed, smaller even than when, as a little girl, she had loitered near with other poor children of the village, waiting till the master of the house should come out and fling them a few pence.

It had happened sometimes in those far-off days that the door had been left wide open and had afforded a view into a dark entrance hall, paved with stone and furnished with stone seats. The children had shouted at this and thrust themselves forward even to the threshold, their voices re-echoing in the interior of the house as in a cave. Then a servant had appeared to drive them away.

"What! You here, too, Maria Maddalena! Aren't you ashamed to go running about with those boys, a grown-up girl like you?"

And she, the girl, had shrunk back abashed, but nevertheless she had turned to stare curiously at the mysterious inside of the house. And just so did she shrink back now and move away, wringing her hands in despair and staring again at the little door which had swallowed up her Paul like a trap. But as she retraced her steps and walked homeward again she began to regret that she had not shouted, that she had not thrown stones at the door and compelled those inside to open it and let her try to rescue her son. She repented her weakness, stood still, irresolute, turned back, then homewards again, drawn this way and that by her tormenting anxiety, uncertain what to do: until at last the instinct of self-preservation, the need of collecting her thoughts and concentrating her strength for the decisive battle, drove her home as a wounded animal takes refuge in its lair.

The instant she got inside the presbytery she shut the door and sat down heavily on the bottom stair. From the top of the staircase came the dim flickering light of the lamp, and everything within the little house, up to now as steady and quiet as a nest built in some crevice of the rocks, seemed to swing from side to side: the rock was shaken to its foundations and the nest was falling to the ground.

Outside the wind moaned and whistled more loudly still; the devil was destroying the presbytery, the church, the whole world of Christians.

"Oh Lord, oh Lord!" wailed the mother, and her voice sounded like the voice of some other woman speaking.

Then she looked at her own shadow on the staircase wall and nodded to it. Truly, she felt that she was not alone, and she began to talk as though another person were there with her, listening and replying.

"What can I do to save him?"

"Wait here till he comes in, and then speak to him plainly and firmly whilst you are still in time, Maria Maddalena."

"But he would get angry and deny it all. It would be better to go to the Bishop and beg him to send us away from this place of perdition. The Bishop is a man of God and knows the world. I will kneel at his feet; I can almost see him now, dressed all in white, sitting in his red reception room, with his golden cross shining on his breast and two fingers raised in benediction. He looks like our Lord Himself! I shall say to him: *Monsignore*, you know that the parish of Aar, besides being the poorest in the kingdom, lies under a curse. For nearly a hundred years it was without a priest and the inhabitants forgot God entirely; then at last a priest came here, but Monsignore knows what manner of man he was. Good and holy till he was fifty years of age: he restored the presbytery and the church, built a bridge across the river at his own expense, and went out shooting and shared the common life of the shepherds and hunters. Then suddenly he changed and became as evil as the devil. He practised sorcery. He began to drink and grew overbearing and passionate. He used to smoke a pipe and swear, and he would sit on the ground playing cards with the worst ruffians of the place, who liked him and protected him, however, and for this very reason the others let him alone. Then, during his latter years, he shut himself up in the presbytery all alone without even a servant, and he never went outside the door except to say Mass, but he always said it before dawn, so that nobody ever went. And they say he used to celebrate when he was drunk. His parishioners were too frightened to bring any accusation against him, because it was said that he was protected by the devil in person. And then when he fell ill there was not a woman who would go and nurse him. Neither woman nor man, of the decent sort, went to help him through his last days, and yet at night every window in the presbytery was lighted up; and the people said that during those last nights the devil had dug an underground passage from this house to the river, through which to carry away the mortal remains of the priest. And by this passage the spirit of the priest used to come back in the years that followed his death and haunt the presbytery, so that no other priest would ever come to live here. A priest used to come from another village every Sunday to say Mass and bury the dead, but one night the spirit of the dead priest destroyed the bridge, and after that for ten years the parish was without a priest, until my Paul came. And I came with him. We found the village and its inhabitants grown quite wild and uncivilized, without faith at all, but everything revived again after my Paul came, like the earth at the return of the spring. But the superstitious were right, disaster will fall upon the new priest because the spirit of the old one still reigns in the presbytery. Some say that he is not dead and that he lives in an underground dwelling communicating with the river. I myself have never believed in such tales, nor have I ever heard any noises. For seven years we have lived here, my Paul and I, as in a little convent. Until a short time ago Paul led the life of an innocent child, he studied and prayed and lived only for the good of his parishioners. Sometimes he used to play the flute. He was not merry by nature, but he was calm and quiet. Seven years of peace and plenty have we had, like those in the Bible. My Paul never drank, he did not go out shooting, he did not smoke and he never looked at a woman. All the money he could save he put aside to rebuild the bridge below the village. He is twenty-eight years old, is my Paul, and now the curse has fallen upon him. A woman has caught him in her net. Oh, my Lord Bishop, send us away from here; save my Paul, for otherwise he will lose his soul as did the former priest! And the woman must be saved, too. After all, she is a woman living alone and she has her temptations also in that lonely house, midst the desolation of this little village where there is nobody fit to bear her company. My Lord Bishop, your Lordship knows that woman, you were her guest with all your following when you came here on your pastoral visitation. There is room and stuff to spare, in that house! And the woman is rich, independent, alone, too much alone! She has brothers and a sister, but they are all far away, married and living in other countries. She remained here alone to look after the house and the property, and she seldom goes out. And until a little while ago my Paul did not even know her. Her father was a strange sort of man, half gentleman, half peasant, a hunter and a heretic. He was a friend of the old priest, and I need say no more. He never went to church, but during his last illness he sent for my Paul, and my Paul stayed with him till he died and gave him a funeral such as had never been seen in these parts. Every single person in the village went to it, even the babies were carried in their mothers' arms. Then afterwards my Paul went on visiting the only survivor of that household. And this orphan girl lives alone with bad servants. Who directs her, who advises her? Who is there to help her if we do not?"

Then the other woman asked her: "Are you certain of this, Maria Maddalena? Are you really sure that what you think is true? Can you actually go before the Bishop and speak thus about your son and that other person, and prove it? And suppose it should not be true?".

"Oh Lord, oh Lord!"

She buried her face in her hands, and immediately there rose before her the vision of her Paul and the woman together in a ground-floor room in the old house. It was a very large room looking out into the orchard, with a domed ceiling, and the floor was of pounded cement with which small sea-shells and pebbles had been mixed; on one side was an immense fireplace, to right and left of which stood an arm-chair and in front was an antique sofa. The whitewashed walls were adorned with arms, stags' heads and antlers, and paintings whose blackened canvases hung in tatters, little of the subjects being distinguishable in the shadows save here and there a dusky hand, some vestige of a face, of a woman's hair, or bunch of fruit.

Paul and the woman were seated in front of the fire, clasping each other's hands.

"Oh, my God!" came the mother's moaning cry.

And in order to banish that diabolic vision she evoked another. It was the same room again, but illumined now by the greenish light that came through the barred window looking out over the meadow and the door which opened direct from the room into the orchard, and through which she saw the trees and foliage gleaming, still wet with the autumn dew. Some fallen leaves were blown softly about the floor and the chains of the antique brass lamp that stood upon the mantelshelf swung to and fro in the draught. Through a half-open door on the other side she could see other rooms, all somewhat dark and with closed windows.

She stood there waiting, with a present of fruit which her Paul had sent to the mistress of the house. And then the mistress came, with a quickened step and yet a little shy; she came from the dark rooms, dressed in black, her pale face framed between two great knots of black plaits, and her thin white hands emerging from the shadows like those in the pictures on the wall.

And even when she came close and stood in the full light of the room there was about her small slender figure something evanescent, doubtful. Her large dark eyes fell instantly on the basket of fruit standing on the table, then turned with a searching look upon the woman who stood waiting, and a swift smile, half joy, half contempt, passed over the sad and sensual curves of her lips.

And in that moment, though she knew not how or why, the first suspicion stirred in the mother's heart.

She could not have explained the reason why, but her memory dwelt on the eagerness with which the girl had welcomed her, making her sit down beside her and asking for news of Paul. She called him Paul as a sister might have done, but she did not treat her as though she were their common mother, but rather as a rival who must be flattered and deceived. She ordered coffee for her, which was served on a large silver tray by a barefoot maid whose face was swathed like an Arab's. She talked of her two brothers, both influential men living far away, taking secret delight in picturing herself between these two, as between columns supporting the fabric of her solitary life. And then at last she led the visitor out to see the orchard, through the door opening straight from the room.

Big purple figs covered with a silver sheen, pears, and great bunches of golden grapes hung amidst the vivid green of the trees and vines. Why should Paul send a gift of fruit to one who possessed so much already?

Even now, sitting on the stairs in the dim light of the flickering lamp, the mother could see again the look, at once ironical and tender, which the girl had turned upon her as she bade her farewell, and the manner in which she lowered her heavy eyelids as though she knew no other way of hiding the feelings her eyes betrayed too plainly. And those eyes, and that way of revealing her soul in a sudden flash of truth and then instantly drawing back into herself again, was extraordinarily like Paul. So much so that during the days following, when because of his manner and his reserve her suspicions grew and filled her heart with fear, she did not think with any hatred of the woman who was leading him into sin, but she thought only of how she might save her too, as though it had been the saving of a daughter of her own.

Autumn and winter had passed without anything happening to confirm her suspicions, but now with the return of the spring, with the blowing of the March winds, the devil took up his work again.

Paul went out at night, and he went to the old house.

"What shall I do, how can I save him?"

But the wind only mocked at her in reply, shaking the house door with its furious blasts.

She remembered their first coming to the village, immediately after Paul had been appointed parish priest here. For twenty years she had been in service and had resisted every temptation, every prompting and instinct of nature, depriving herself of love, even of bread itself, in order that she might bring up her boy rightly and set him a good example. Then they came here, and just such a furious wind as this had beset them on their journey. It had been springtime then, too, but the whole valley seemed to have slipped back into the grip of winter. Leaves were blown hither and thither, the trees bent before the blast, leaning one against another, as though gazing fearfully at the battalions of black clouds driving rapidly across the sky from all parts of the horizon, while large hailstones fell and bruised the tender green.

At the point where the road turns, overlooking the valley, and then descends towards the river, there was such a sudden onslaught of wind that the horses came to a dead stop, pricking their ears and neighing with fear. The storm shook their bridles like some bandit who had seized their heads to stop them that he might rob the travellers, and even Paul, although apparently he was enjoying the adventure, had cried out with vague superstition in his voice: "It must be the evil spirit of the old priest trying to prevent us coming here!".

But his words were lost in the shrill whistling of the wind, and although he smiled a little ruefully, a one-sided smile that touched but one corner of his lips, his eyes were sad as they rested on the village which now came in sight, like a picture hanging on the green hill-side on the opposite slope of the valley beyond the tumbling stream.

The wind dropped a little after they had crossed the river. The people of the village, who were as ready to welcome the new priest as though he were the Messiah, were all gathered together in the piazza before the church, and on a sudden impulse a group of the younger men amongst them had gone down to meet the travellers on the river bank. They descended the hill like a flight of young eagles from the mountains, and the air resounded with their merry shouts. When they reached their parish priest they gathered round him and bore him up the hill in triumph, every now and then firing their guns into the air as a mark of rejoicing. The whole valley echoed with their cheering and firing, the wind itself was pacified and the weather began to clear up.

Even in this present hour of anguish the mother's heart swelled with pride when she recalled that other hour of triumph. Again she seemed to be living in a dream, to be borne as though on a cloud by those noisy youths, while beside her walked her Paul, so boyish still, but with a look half divine upon his face as those strong men bowed before him with respect.

Up and up they climbed. Fireworks were being let off on the highest and barest point of the ridge, the flames streaming out like red banners against the background of black clouds and casting their reflections on the grey village, the green hill-side and the tamarisks and elder trees that bordered the path.

Up and still up they went. Over the parapet of the piazza, leaned another wall of human bodies and eager faces crowned with men's caps or framed in women's kerchiefs with long fluttering fringes.

The children's eyes danced with delight at the unwonted excitement, and on the edge of the ridge the figures of the boys tending the fireworks looked like slender black demons in the distance.

Through the wide-open door of the church the flames of the lighted candles could be seen trembling like narcissi in the wind; the bells were ringing loudly, and even the clouds in the pale silvery sky seemed to have gathered round the tower to watch and wait.

Suddenly a cry rang out from the little crowd: "Here he is! Here he is!... And he looks like a saint!".

There was nothing of a saint about him, however, except that air of utter calm: he did not speak, he did not even acknowledge the people's greetings, he seemed in no way moved by that popular demonstration: he only pressed his lips tightly together and bent his eyes upon the ground with a slight frown, as though tired by the burden of that heavy brow. Then suddenly, when they had reached the piazza, and were surrounded by the welcoming throng, the mother saw him falter as though about to fall, a man supported him for an instant, then immediately he recovered his balance and turning swiftly into the church he fell on his knees before the altar and began to intone the evening prayer.

And the weeping women gave the responses.

The poor women wept, but their tears were the happy tears of love and hope and the longing for a joy not of this world, and the mother felt the balm of those tears falling on her heart even in this hour of her grief. Her Paul! Her love, her hope, the embodiment of her desire for unearthly joy! And now the spirit of evil was drawing him away, and she sat there at the bottom of the staircase as at the bottom of a well, and made no effort to rescue him.

She felt she was suffocating, her heart was heavy as a stone. She got up in order to breathe more easily, and mounting the stairs she picked up the lamp and held it aloft as she looked round her bare little room, where a wooden bedstead and a worm-eaten wardrobe kept each other company as the only furniture in the place. It was a room fit only for a servant – she had never desired to better her lot – content to find her only wealth in being the mother of her Paul.

Then she went into his room with its white walls and the narrow virginal bed. This chamber had once been kept as simple and tidy as that of a girl; he had loved quiet, silence, order, and always had flowers upon his little writing-table in front of the window. But latterly he had not cared about anything: he had left his drawers and cupboards open and his books littered about on the chairs or even on the floor.

The water in which he had washed before going out exhaled a strong scent of roses: a coat had been flung off carelessly and lay on the floor like a prostrate shadow of himself. That sight and that scent roused the mother from her preoccupation: she picked up the coat and thought scornfully that she would be strong enough even to pick up her son himself. Then she tidied the room, clattering to and fro without troubling now to deaden the sound of her heavy peasant shoes. She drew up to the table the leather chair in which he sat to read, thumping it down on the floor as though ordering it to remain in its place awaiting the speedy return of its master. Then she turned to the little mirror hanging beside the window...

Mirrors are forbidden in a priest's house, he must forget that he has a body. On this point, at least, the old priest had observed the law, and from the road he could have been seen shaving himself by the open window, behind the panes of which he had hung a black cloth to throw up the reflection. But Paul, on the contrary, was attracted to the mirror as to a well from whose depths a face smiled up at him, luring him down to perish. But it was the mother's own scornful face and threatening eyes that the little mirror reflected now, and with rising anger she put out her hand and tore it from its nail. Then she flung the window wide open and let the wind blow in to purify the room: the books and papers on the table seemed to come alive, twisting and circling into every corner, the fringe of the bed-cover shook and waved and the flame of the lamp flickered almost to extinction.

She gathered up the books and papers and replaced them on the table. Then she noticed an open Bible, with a coloured picture that she greatly admired, and she bent down to examine it more closely. There was Jesus the Good Shepherd watering His sheep at a spring in the midst of a forest. Between the trees, against the background of blue sky, could be seen a distant city, red in the light of the setting sun, a holy city, the City of Salvation.

There had been a time when he used to study far into the night; the stars over the ridge looked in at his window and the nightingales sang him their plaintive notes. For the first year after they came to the village he often talked of leaving and going back into the world: then he settled down into a sort of waking sleep, in the shadow of the ridge and the murmur of the trees. Thus seven years passed, and his mother never suggested they should move elsewhere, for they were so happy in the little village that seemed to her the most beautiful in all the world, because her Paul was its saviour and its king.

She closed the window and replaced the mirror, which showed her now her own face grown white and drawn, her eyes dim with tears. Again she asked herself if perhaps she were not mistaken. She turned towards a crucifix which hung on the wall above a kneeling-stool, raising the lamp above her head that she might see it better; and midst the shadows that her movements threw on the wall it seemed as though the Christ, thin and naked, stretched upon the Cross, bowed His head to hear her prayer. And great tears coursed down her face and fell upon her dress, heavy as tears of blood.

"Lord, save us all! Save Thou me, even me. Thou Who hangest there pale and bloodless, Thou Whose Face beneath its crown of thorns is sweet as a wild rose, Thou Who art above our wretched passions, save us all!"

Then she hurried out of the room and went downstairs. She passed through the tiny dining-room, where drowsy flies, startled by the lamp, buzzed heavily round and the howling wind and swaying trees outside beat like rain upon the small, high window and thence into the kitchen, where she sat down before the fire, already banked up with cinders for the night. Even there the wind seemed to penetrate by every crack and cranny, so that instead of being in the long low kitchen, whose uneven ceiling was supported by smoke-blackened beams and rafters, she felt as if she were in a rocking boat adrift on a stormy sea. And although determined to wait up for her son and begin the battle at once, she still fought against conviction and tried to persuade herself that she was mistaken.

She felt it unjust that God should send her such sorrow, and she went back over her past life, day by day, trying to find some reason for her present unhappiness; but all her days had passed hard and clean as the beads of the rosary she held in her shaking fingers. She had done no wrong, unless perchance sometimes in her thoughts.

She saw herself again as an orphan in the house of poor relations, in that same village, ill-treated by everyone, toiling barefoot, bearing heavy burdens on her head, washing clothes in the river, or carrying corn to the mill. An elderly man, a relative of hers, was employed by the miller, and each time she went down to the mill, if there was nobody to see him, he followed her into the bushes and tufts of tamarisk and kissed her by force, pricking her face with his bristly beard and covering her with flour. When she told of this, the aunts with whom she lived would not let her go to the mill again. Then one day the man, who ordinarily never came up to the village, suddenly appeared at the house and said he wished to marry the girl. The other members of the family laughed at him, slapped him on the back and brushed the flour off his coat with a broom. But he took no notice of their jests and kept his eyes fixed on the girl. At last she consented to marry him, but she continued to live with her relations and went down each day to the mill to see her husband, who always gave her a small measure of flour unknown to his master. Then one day as she was going home with her apron full of flour she felt something move beneath it. Startled, she dropped the corners of her apron and all the flour was scattered, and she was so giddy that she had to sit down on the ground. She thought it was an earthquake, the houses rocked before her eyes, the path went up and down and she flung herself prone on the floury grass. Then she got up and ran home laughing, yet afraid, for she knew she was with child.

She was left a widow before her Paul was old enough to talk, but his bright baby eyes followed her everywhere, and she had mourned for her husband as for a good old man who had been kind to her, but nothing more. She was soon consoled, however, for a cousin proposed that they should go together to the town and there take service.

"In that way you will be able to support your boy, and later on you can send for him and put him to school."

And so she worked and lived only for him.

She had lacked neither the occasion nor the inclination to indulge in pleasures, if not in sin. Master and servants, peasant and townsman, all had tried to catch her as once the old kinsman had caught her amongst the tamarisks. Man is a hunter and woman his prey, but she had succeeded in evading all pitfalls and keeping herself pure and good, since she already looked on herself as the mother of a priest. Then wherefore now this chastisement, O Lord?

She bowed her weary head and the tears rolled down her face and fell on the rosary in her lap.

Gradually she grew drowsy, and confused memories floated through her mind. She thought she was in the big warm kitchen of the Seminary, where she had been servant for ten years and where she had succeeded in getting her Paul admitted as student. Black figures went silently to and fro, and in the passage outside she could hear the smothered laughter and larking the boys indulged in when there was nobody to reprove them. Tired to death, she sat beside a window opening on to a dark yard, a duster on her lap, but too weary to move so much as a finger towards her work. In the dream, too, she was waiting for Paul, who had slipped out of the Seminary secretly without telling her where he was going.

"If they find out they will expel him at once" she thought, and she waited anxiously till the house was quite quiet that she might let him in without being observed.

Suddenly she awoke and found herself back in the narrow presbytery kitchen, shaken by the wind like a ship at sea, but the impression of the dream was so strong that she felt on her lap for the duster and listened for the smothered laughter of the boys knocking each other about in the passage. Then in a moment reality gripped her again, and she thought Paul must have come in while she was fast asleep and thus succeeded in escaping her notice. And actually, midst all the creaking and shaking caused by the wind, she could hear steps inside the house: someone was coming downstairs, crossing the ground-floor rooms, entering the kitchen. She thought she was still dreaming when a short, stout priest, with a week's growth of beard upon his chin, stood before her and looked her in the face with a smile. The few teeth he had left were blackened with too much smoking, his light-coloured eyes pretended to be fierce – she could tell that he was really laughing, and immediately she knew him for the former priest – but still she did not feel afraid.

"It is only a dream" she told herself, but in reality she knew she only said that to give herself courage and that it was no phantom, but a fact.

"Sit down" she said, moving her stool aside to make room for him in front of the fire. He sat down and drew up his cassock a little, exhibiting a pair of discoloured and worn blue stockings.

"Since you are sitting here doing nothing, you might mend my stockings for me, Maria Maddalena: I have no woman to look after me" he said simply. And she thought to herself: "Can this be the terrible priest? That shows I am still dreaming".

And then she tried to make him betray himself.

"If you are dead you have no need of stockings" she said.

"How do you know I am dead? I am very much alive, on the contrary, and sitting here. And before long I am going to drive both you and your son out of my parish. It was a bad thing for you, coming here, you had better have brought him up to follow his father's trade. But you are an ambitious woman, and you wanted to come back as mistress where you had lived as a servant: so now you will see what you have gained by it!"

"We will go away" she answered humbly and sadly. "Indeed, I want to go. Man or ghost, whatever you are, have patience for a few days and we shall be gone."

"And where can you go?" said the old priest. "Wherever you go it will be the same thing. Take rather the advice of one who knows what he is talking about and let your Paul follow his destiny. Let him know the woman, otherwise the same thing will befall him that befell me. When I was young I would have nothing to do with women, nor with any other kind of pleasure. I only thought of winning Paradise, and I failed to perceive that Paradise is here on earth. When I did perceive it, it was too late: my arm could no longer reach up to gather the fruit of the tree and my knees would not bend that I might quench my thirst at the spring. So then I began to drink wine, to smoke a pipe and to play cards with all the rascals of the place. You call them rascals, but I call them honest lads who enjoy life as they find it. It does one good to be in their company, it diffuses a little warmth and merriment, like the company of boys on a holiday. The only difference is that it is always holiday for them, and therefore they are even merrier and more careless than the boys, who cannot forget that they must soon go back to school."

While he was talking thus the mother thought to herself: "He is only saying these things in order to persuade me to leave my Paul alone and let him be damned. He has been sent by his friend and master, the Devil, and I must be on my guard".

Yet, in spite of herself, she listened to him readily and found herself almost agreeing with what he said. She reflected that, in spite of all her efforts, Paul too might 'take a holiday' and instinctively her mother's heart instantly sought excuses for him.

"You may be right" she said with increased sadness and humility, which now, however, was partly pretence. "I am only a poor, ignorant woman and don't understand very much: but one thing I am sure of, that God sent us into the world to suffer."

"God sent us into the world to enjoy it. He sends suffering to punish us for not having understood how to enjoy, and that is the truth, you fool of a woman! God created the world with all its beauty and gave it to man for his pleasure: so much the worse for him if he does not understand! But why should I trouble to explain this to you? All I mind about is turning you out of this place, you and your Paul, and so much the worse for you if you want to stop!"

"We are going, never fear, we are going very soon. That I can promise you, for it's my wish, too."

"You only say that because you are afraid of me. But you are wrong to be afraid. You think that it was I who prevented your feet from walking and your matches from striking: and perhaps it was I, but that is not to say that I mean any harm to you or your Paul. I only want you to go away. And mind, if you do not keep your word you will be sorry! Well, you will see me again and I shall remind you of this conversation. Meanwhile, I will leave you my stockings to mend."

"Very well, I will mend them."

"Then shut your eyes, for I don't choose that you should see my bare legs. Ha, ha!" he laughed, pulling off one shoe with the toe of the other and bending down to draw off his stockings, "no woman has ever seen my bare flesh, however much they have slandered me, and you are too old and ugly to be the first. Here is one stocking, and here is the other; I shall come and fetch them soon..."

She opened her eyes with a start. She was alone again, in the kitchen with the wind howling round it.

"O Lord, what a dream!" she murmured with a sigh. Nevertheless, she stooped to look for the stockings, and she thought she heard the faint footfall of the ghost as it passed out of the kitchen, vanishing through the closed door.

When Paul left the woman's house and found himself out in the meadow again he too had the sensation that there was something alive, something ghostly, undefinable in the wind. It buffeted him about and chilled him through and through after his ardent dream of love, and as it twisted and flattened his coat against his body he thought with a quiver of the woman clinging to him in a passionate embrace.

When he turned the corner by the church the fury of the wind forced him to stop for a moment, with head bent before the blast, one hand holding on his hat and the other clutching his coat together. He had no breath left, and giddiness overcame him as it had overcome his young mother that far-off day on the way from the mill.

And with mingled excitement and loathing he felt that something terrible and great was born in him at that moment: for the first time he realized clearly and unmistakably that he loved Agnes with an earthly love, and that he gloried in this love.

Until a few hours ago he had been under a delusion, persuading both himself and her that his love was purely spiritual. But he had to admit that it was she who had first let her gaze linger upon him, that from their earliest meeting her eyes had sought his with a look that implored his help and his love. And little by little he had yielded to the fascination of that appeal, had been drawn to her by pity, and the solitude that surrounded her had brought them together.

And after their eyes had met their hands had sought and found each other, and that night they had kissed. And now his blood, which had flowed quietly so many years, rushed through his veins like liquid fire and the weak flesh yielded, at once the vanquished and the victor.

The woman had proposed that they two should secretly leave the village and live or die together. In the intoxication of the moment he had agreed to the proposal and they were to meet again the following night to settle their plans. But now the reality of the outside world, and that wind that seemed trying to strip him bare, tore away the veil of self-deception. Breathless, he stood before the church door; he was icy cold, and felt as though he were standing naked there in the midst of the little village, and that all his poor parishioners, sleeping the sleep of the weary, were beholding him thus in their dreams, naked, and black with sin.

Yet all the time he was thinking how best to plan his flight with the woman. She had told him that she possessed much money... Then suddenly he felt impelled to go back to her that instant and dissuade her: he actually walked a few steps beside the wall where his mother had passed shortly before, then turned back in despair and fell on his knees in front of the church door and leaned his head against it, crying low, "Oh God, save me!" and his black cloak was blown flapping about his shoulders as he knelt there, like a vulture nailed alive upon the door.

His whole soul was fighting savagely, with a violence greater even than that of the wind on those high hills; it was the supreme struggle of the blind instinct of the flesh against the dominion of the spirit.

After a few moments he rose to his feet, uncertain still which of the two had conquered. But his mind was clearer and he recognized the real nature of his motives, confessing to himself that what swayed him most, more than the fear and the love of God, more than the desire for promotion and the hatred of sin, was his terror of the consequences of an open scandal.

The realization that he judged himself so mercilessly encouraged him to hope still for salvation. But at the bottom of his heart he knew he was henceforth bound to that woman as to life itself, that her image would be with him in his house, that he would walk at her side by day and at night sleep entangled in the inextricable meshes of her long dark hair. And beneath his sorrow and remorse, deeper and stronger still, he felt a tumult of joy glow through his inmost being as a subterranean fire burns within the earth.

Directly he opened the presbytery door he perceived the streak of light that issued from the kitchen and shone across the little dining-room into the entrance hall. Then he saw his mother sitting by the dead ashes, as though watching by a corpse, and with a pang of grief, a grief that never left him again, he instantly knew the whole truth.

He followed the streak of light through the little dining-room, faltered a second at the kitchen door, and then advanced to the hearth with hands outstretched as though to save himself from falling.

"Why have you not gone to bed?" he asked curtly.

His mother turned to look at him, her dream-haunted face still deathly pale; yet she was steady and quiet, almost stern, and while her eyes sought those of her son, his tried to evade her gaze.

"I was waiting up for you, Paul. Where have you been?"

He knew instinctively that every word that was not strictly true would be only a useless farce between them; yet he was forced to lie to her.

"I have been with a sick person" he replied quickly.

For an instant his deep voice seemed to disperse the evil dream; for an instant only, and the mother's face was transfigured with joy. Then the shadow fell again on face and heart.

"Paul," she said gently, lowering her eyes with a feeling of shame, but with no hesitation in her speech, "Paul, come nearer to me, I have something to say to you."

And although he moved no nearer to her, she went on speaking in a low voice, as though close to his ear: "I know where you have been. For many nights now I have heard you go out, and tonight I followed you and saw where you went. Paul, think of what you are doing!".

He did not answer, made no sign that he had heard. His mother raised her eyes and beheld him standing tall and straight above her, pale as death, his shadow cast by the lamp upon the wall behind him, motionless as though transfixed upon a cross. And she longed for him to cry out and reproach her, to protest his innocence.

But he was remembering his soul's appeal as he knelt before the church door, and now God had heard his cry and had sent his own mother to him to save him. He wanted to bow before her, to fall at her knee and implore her to lead him away from the village, then and there, immediately; and at the same time he was shaking with rage and humiliation, humiliation at finding his weakness exposed, rage at having been watched and followed. Yet he grieved for the sorrow he was causing her. Then suddenly he remembered that he had not only to save himself, but to save appearances also.

"Mother," he said, going close to her and placing his hand on her head, "I tell you that I have been with someone who is ill."

"There is nobody ill in that house."

"Not all sick persons are in bed."

"Then in that case you yourself are more ill than the woman you went to see, and you must take care of yourself. Paul, I am only an ignorant woman, but I am your mother, and I tell you that sin is an illness worse than any other, because it attacks the soul. Moreover," she added, taking his hand and drawing him down towards her that he might hear her better, "it is not yourself only that you have to save, O child of God... remember that you must not destroy her soul... nor bring her to harm in this life either."

He was bending over her, but at these words he shot upright again like a steel spring. His mother had cut him to the quick. Yes, it was true; during all that hour of perturbation since he had quitted the woman he had thought only of himself.

He tried to withdraw his hand from his mother's, so hard and cold, but she grasped it so imperatively that he felt as though he had been arrested and were being led bound to prison. Then his thoughts turned again to God; it was God who had bound him, therefore he must submit to be led, but nevertheless he felt the rebellion and desperation of the guilty prisoner who sees no way of escape.

"Leave me alone," he said roughly, dragging his hand away by force, "I am no longer a boy and know myself what is good or bad for me!"

Then the mother felt as though she were turned to stone, for he had practically confessed his fault.

"No, Paul, you don't see the wrong you have done. If you did see it you would not speak like that."

"Then how should I speak?"

"You would not shout like that, but you would assure me there is nothing wrong between you and that woman. But that is just what you don't tell me, because you cannot do so conscientiously, and therefore it is better you should say nothing at all. Don't speak! I don't ask it of you now, but think well what you are about, Paul."

Paul made no reply, but moved slowly from his mother's side and stood in the middle of the kitchen waiting for her to go on speaking.

"Paul, I have nothing more to say to you, and I have no wish to say anything more. But I shall talk with God about you."

Then he sprang back to her side with blazing eyes as though he were about to strike her.

"Enough!" he cried. "You will be wise never to speak of this again, neither to me nor to anyone else; and keep your fancies to yourself!"

She rose to her feet, stern and resolute, seized him by the arms and forced him to look her straight in the eyes; then she let him go and sat down again, her hands gripping each other tightly in her lap.

Paul moved towards the door, then turned and began to walk up and down the kitchen. The moaning of the wind outside made an accompaniment to the rustle of his clothes, which was like the rustle of a woman's dress, for he wore a cassock made of silk and his cloak was of the very finest material. And in that moment of indecision, when he felt himself caught in a whirlpool of conflicting emotions, even that silken rustle seemed to speak and warn him that henceforth his life would be but a maze of errors and light things and vileness. Everything spoke to him; the wind outside, that recalled the long loneliness of his youth, and inside the house the mournful figure of his mother, the sound of his own steps, the sight of his own shadow on the floor. To and fro he walked, to and fro, treading on his shadow as he sought to overcome and stamp down his own self. He thought with pride that he had no need of any supernatural aid, such as he had invoked to save him, and then immediately this pride filled him with terror.

"Get up and go to bed" he said, coming back to his mother's side; and then, seeing that she did not move but sat with head bowed as though asleep, he bent down to look more closely in her face and perceived that she was weeping silently.

"Mother!"

"No," she said, without moving, "I shall never mention this thing to you again, neither to you nor to anyone else. But I shall not stir from this place except to leave the presbytery and the village, never to return, unless you swear to me that you will never set foot in that house again."

He raised himself from his bending position, overtaken again by that feeling of giddiness, and again superstition took hold of him, urging him to promise whatever his mother asked of him, since it was God Himself who was speaking by her mouth. And simultaneously a flood of bitter words rose to his lips, and he wanted to cry out upon his mother, to throw the blame on her and reproach her for having brought him from his native village and set his feet upon a way that was not his. But what would be the use? She would not even understand. Well, well!... With one hand he made a gesture as though brushing away the shadows from before his eyes, then suddenly he stretched out this hand over his mother's head, and in his imagination saw his opened fingers extend in luminous rays above her: "Mother, I swear to you that I will never enter that house again".

And immediately he left the kitchen, feeling that here was the end of everything. He was saved. But as he crossed the adjoining dining-room he heard his mother weeping unrestrainedly, as though she were weeping for the dead.

Back in his room, the scent of roses and the sight of the various objects strewn about which were associated with his passion, impregnated and coloured by it, as it were, shook him afresh. He moved here and there without any reason, opened the window and thrust his head out into the wind, feeling as helpless as one of the million leaves whirled about in space, now in the dark shadow, now in the bright light of the moon, playthings of the winds and clouds. At last he drew himself up and closed the window, saying aloud as he did so: "Let us be men!".

He stood erect to his full height, numb as though all his body were cold and hard and enclosed in an armour of pride. He desired no more to feel the sensations of the flesh, nor the sorrow nor the joy of sacrifice, nor the sadness of his loneliness; he had no wish even to kneel before God and receive the word of approval granted to the willing servant. He asked nothing from anyone; he wanted only to go forward in the straight way, alone and hopeless. Yet he was afraid of going to bed and putting out the light, and instead he sat down and began to read St. Paul's Epistle to the Corinthians: but the printed words fled his gaze, they swelled and shrank and danced up and down before his eyes. Why had his mother wept so bitterly, after he had sworn an oath to her? What could she have understood? Ah, yes, she understood; the mother's heart understood only too well the mortal anguish of her son, his renunciation of life itself.

Suddenly a wave of red overspread his face, and he raised his head, listening to the wind.

"There was no need to have sworn," he said to himself with a doubtful smile "the really strong man never swears. Whoever takes an oath, as I did, is also ready to break his oath, even as I am ready."

And instantly he knew that the struggle was only really beginning, and so great was his consternation that he rose from his seat and went to look at himself in the mirror.

"Here thou standest, the man appointed by God, and if thou wilt not give thyself wholly to Him, then the spirit of evil will take possession of thee for ever."

Then he staggered to his narrow bed and, dressed as he was, flung himself down upon it and burst into tears. He wept silently that his mother might not hear him, and that he might not hear his own crying, but his heart within him cried aloud and he was wrung with inward grief.

"Oh God, take me, bring me out of this!"

And the uttered words brought him real relief, as though he had found a plank of salvation in the midst of that sea of sorrow.

The crisis over he began to reflect. Everything seemed clear to him now, like a landscape seen from a window in the full light of the sun. He was a priest, he believed in God, he had wedded the Church and was vowed to chastity, he was like a married man and had no right to betray his wife. Why he had fallen in love with that woman and still loved her he did not exactly know.

Perhaps he had reached a sort of physical crisis, when the youth and strength of his twenty-eight years awoke suddenly from its prolonged sleep and yearned towards Agnes because she had the closest affinity with him, and because she too, no longer very young, had like him been deprived of life and love, shut up in her house as in a convent.

Thus from the very first it had been love masquerading as friendship. They had been caught in a net of smiles and glances, and the very impossibility of there being any question of love between them drew them together: nobody entertained the faintest suspicion of their relationship to each other, and they met without emotion, without fear and without desire. Yet little by little desire crept into that love of theirs, chaste and pure as a pool of still water beneath a wall that suddenly crumbles and falls in ruins.

All these things passed through his mind as he probed deep into his conscience and found the truth. He knew that from the first glance he had desired the woman, from the first glance he had possessed her in his heart, and all the rest had been only self-deception whereby he had sought to justify himself in his own eyes.

Thus it was, and he was forced to acknowledge the truth. Thus it was, because it is man's nature to suffer, to love, to find his mate and have her and to suffer again; to do good and receive it, to do evil and receive it, this is the life of man. Yet all his reflections lifted not one iota of the anguish that weighed upon his heart; and now he comprehended the true meaning of that anguish: it was the bitterness of death, for to renounce love and the possession of Agnes was to renounce life itself. Then his thoughts went further: "Was not even this vain and futile? When the momentary pleasure of love is past, the spirit resumes mastery over itself, and, with a more intense longing for solitude than before, it takes refuge again within its prison-house, the mortal body that clothes it. Why, therefore, should he be made unhappy by this loneliness? Had he not accepted and endured it for so many years, all the best years of his life? Even supposing he could really escape with Agnes and marry her, would he not always be alone within himself just the same...?".

Yet the mere fact of pronouncing her name, the bare idea of the possibility of living with her, made him spring up in a fever of excitement. In imagination again he saw her stretched beside him, in imagination he held out his arms to draw her close to him, slender and supple as a reed in the stream; he whispered sweet words into the little hollow behind her ear, covered his face with her loosened hair, warm and scented like the flowers of the wild saffron. And biting hard into his pillow, he repeated to her all the Song of Songs, and when this was ended he told her he would come back to her the next day, that he was glad to grieve his mother and his God, glad that he had sworn an oath and given himself over to remorse, to superstition and to fear, for now he could break loose from everything and return to her.

Then he grew calmer and began to reflect again.

As a sick man is relieved to know at least the nature of his malady, so Paul would have been relieved to know at least why all these things had befallen him, and like his mother, he went over all the story of his past life.

The moaning of the wind outside mingled with his earliest memories, faint and indistinct. He saw himself in a courtyard, where, he did not know, but perhaps the courtyard of the house where his mother was a servant, and he was climbing on the wall with other boys. The top of the wall was edged with pieces of glass as sharp as knives, but this did not prevent the boys from scrambling up to look over, even though they cut their hands. As a matter of fact, there was a certain daring pleasure in wounding themselves, and they showed each other their blood and then dried it beneath their armpits, under the delusion that nobody would notice their cut hands. From the top of the wall they could see nothing except the street, into which they were perfectly free to go; but they preferred climbing on to the wall because that was forbidden, and they amused themselves by throwing stones at the few people who passed and then hiding, their sensations divided between delight in their own boldness and their fear of being discovered. A deaf and dumb girl, who was also a cripple, used to sit by the wood pile at the bottom of the courtyard, and from there she used to watch them with an expression at once imploring and severe in her large dark eyes. The boys were afraid of her, but they did not dare to molest her; on the contrary, they lowered their voices as though she could hear them and sometimes they even invited her to play with them. Then the crippled child used to laugh with an almost insane delight, but she never moved from her corner.

In imagination he saw again those dark eyes, in whose depths the light of sorrow and desire already shone; he saw them far off at the bottom of his memory as at the bottom of that mysterious courtyard, and it seemed to him that they resembled the eyes of Agnes.

Then he saw himself again in that same street where he had thrown stones at the passers-by, but farther down, at the turning of a little lane shut in by a group of dilapidated old houses. His home lay just between the street and the lane, in the house of well-to-do people, all women and all fat and serious; they used to close all doors and windows at dusk and they received no visitors except other women and priests, with whom they used to joke and laugh, but always in a decorous, guarded manner.

It had been one of these priests who had caught him by the shoulders one day, and gripping him firmly between his bony knees and raising his timid face with a vigorous hand, had asked him: "Is it true that you want to be a priest?".

The boy had nodded yes, and having been given a sacred picture and a friendly slap he had remained in a corner of the room listening to the conversation between the priests and the women. They were discussing the parish priest of Aar and describing how he went out hunting and smoked a pipe and let his beard grow, yet how nevertheless the Bishop hesitated to interdict him because he would have great difficulty in finding another priest willing to bury himself in that remote village. Moreover, the easygoing priest in possession threatened to tie up and fling into the river anyone who ventured to try and oust him from his place.

"The worst of it is that the simpletons of Aar are attached to the man, although they are frightened of him and his sorceries.

Some of them actually believe he is the Antichrist, and the women all declare that they will help him to truss up his successor and throw him into the river."

"Do you hear that, Paul? If you become a priest and have any idea of going back to your mother's village, you must look out for a lively time!"

It was a woman who flung this joke at him, Marielena; she was the one who had charge of him, and when she drew him towards her to comb his hair her fat stomach and her soft breast used to make him think she was made of cushions. He was very fond of Marielena; in spite of her corpulent body she had a refined and pretty face, with cheeks softly tinted with pink and gentle brown eyes. He used to look up at her as one looks at the ripe fruit hanging on the tree, and perhaps she had been his first love.

Then came his life at the Seminary. His mother had taken him there one October morning, when the sky was blue and everything smelt of new wine. The road mounted steeply and at the top of the hill was the archway which connected the Seminary with the Bishop's house, curved like a vast frame over the sunny landscape of cottages, trees and granite steps, with the cathedral tower at the bottom of the picture. The grass was springing up between the cobblestones in front of the Bishop's house, several men rode past on horseback and the horses had long legs with hairy fetlocks and were shod with gleaming iron shoes. He noticed all these things because he kept his eyes shyly on the ground, a little ashamed of himself, a little ashamed of his mother. Yes, why not confess it once for all? He had always been more or less ashamed of his mother, because she was a servant and came from that village of poor simpletons. Only later, very much later, had he overcome this ignoble feeling by sheer force of pride and will, and the more he had been unreasonably ashamed of his origin, all the more did he subsequently glory in it to himself and before God choosing voluntarily to live in this miserable hamlet, subjecting himself to his mother, and respecting her most trifling wishes and conforming to her humblest ways.

But the remembrance of his mother as a servant, aye, even less than a servant, a mere drudge in the Seminary kitchen, brought back with it the most humiliating memories of his youth. And yet she worked as a servant for his sake. On the days when he went to confession and communion his Superior obliged him to go and kiss his mother's hand and ask her pardon for the faults he had committed. The hand which she dried hurriedly with a dishcloth smelt of soapsuds and was chapped and wrinkled like an old wall, and he was filled with shame and rage at being forced to kiss it; but he asked forgiveness of God for his inability to ask forgiveness of her.

Thus God had revealed Himself to Paul, as hidden behind his mother in the damp and smoky kitchen of the Seminary: God Who is in every place, in heaven and on earth and in all things created.

And in his hours of exaltation, when he lay in his little room staring with wide-open eyes into the darkness, he had dwelt with wonder on the thought "I shall be a priest, I shall be able to consecrate the host and change it into God." And at those times he thought also of his mother, and when he was away from her and could not see her, he loved her and realized that his own greatness was all due to her, for instead of sending him to herd goats or carry sacks of grain to the mill, as his father had done, she was making him into a priest, one who had power to consecrate the host and change it into God.

It was thus he conceived his mission in life. He knew nothing of the world; his brightest and most emotional memories were the ceremonies of the great religious festivals, and recalling these memories now, in all the bitterness of his present anguish, they awoke in him a sense of light and joy and presented themselves to his mind's eye as great living pictures. And the remembered music of the cathedral organ and the sense of mystery in the ceremonies of Holy Week became part of his present sorrow, of that anguish of life and death which seemed to weigh him down upon his bed as the burden of man's sin had lain upon Christ in the sepulchre.

It was during one of these periods of mystical agitation that for the first time he had come into intimate relations with a woman.

When he thought of it now it seemed like a dream, neither good nor evil, but only strange.

Every holiday he went to visit the women with whom he had lived during his boyhood, and they welcomed him as though he were already a priest, with familiar friendliness and cheerfulness, but always with a certain dignity. When he looked at Marielena he used to blush, and then scorned himself for blushing, because though he still liked her, he now saw her in all her crude realism, fat, soft and shapeless; nevertheless her presence and her gentle eyes still roused little tremors in him.

Marielena and her sisters used often to invite him to dinner on feast days. On one occasion, Palm Sunday, he happened to arrive early, and whilst his hostesses were busy laying the table and awaiting their other guests, Paul went out into their little garden and began to walk up and down the path which ran beside the outer wall, beneath the aspens covered with little golden leaves. The sky was all a milky blue, the air soft and warm with the light wind from the eastern hills, and the cuckoo could already be heard calling in the distance.

Just as he was standing on tiptoe childishly to pick a drop of resin off an almond tree, he suddenly saw a pair of large greenish eyes fixed upon him from the lane on the other side of the garden wall. They looked like the eyes of a cat, and the whole personality of the woman, who was sitting crouched upon the steps of a dark doorway at the end of the lane, had something feline about it. He could conjure up her image again so clearly that he even felt as if he still held the drop of soft resin between his finger and thumb, whilst his fascinated eyes could not withdraw themselves from hers! And over the doorway he remembered a little window surrounded by a white line with a small cross over it. He had known that doorway and that window very well ever since he was a boy, and the cross placed there as a charm against temptation had always amused him, because the woman who lived in the cottage, Maria Paska, was a lost woman. He could see her now before him, with her fringed kerchief showing her white neck, and her long coral ear-rings, like two long drops of blood. With her elbows resting on her knees and her pale, delicate face supported between her hands, Maria Paska looked at him steadily, and at last she smiled at him, but without moving. Her white even teeth and the somewhat cruel expression of her eyes only served to accentuate the feline look about her face. Suddenly, however, she dropped her hands into her lap, raised her head and assumed a grave and sad expression. A big man, with his cap drawn down to hide his face, was coming cautiously down the lane and keeping close in the shadow of the wall.

Then Maria Paska got up quickly and went into the house, and the big man followed her and shut the door.

Paul never forgot his terrible agitation as he walked about in the little garden and thought of those two shut up in that squalid house in the lane. It was a sort of uneasy sadness, a sense of discomfort that made him want to be alone and to hide himself like a sick animal, and during dinner he was unusually silent amidst the cheerful talk of the other guests. Directly dinner was over he returned to the garden: the woman was there, on the look-out again and in the same position as before. The sun never reached the damp corner where her door was, and she looked as if she were so white and delicate because she always lived in the shade.

When she saw the seminarist she did not move, but she smiled at him, and then her face became grave as on the arrival of the big man. She called out to Paul, speaking as one would speak to a young boy: "I say, will you come and bless my house on Saturday? Last year the priest who was going round blessing the houses refused to come into mine. May he go to hell, he and all his bag of tricks!".

Paul made no answer, he felt inclined to throw a stone at the woman, in fact he did pick one up from the wall, but then put it back and wiped his hand on his handkerchief. But all through Holy Week, whilst he was hearing Mass, or taking part in the sacred function, or, taper in hand, escorting the Bishop with all the other seminarists, he always seemed to see the woman's eyes staring at him till it became a veritable obsession. He had wanted to exorcize her, as one possessed of the Devil, yet at the same time he felt somehow that the spirit of evil was within himself. During the ceremony of feet-washing, when the Bishop stooped before the twelve beggars (who looked as though they might really have been the twelve apostles), Paul's heart was moved by the thought that on the Saturday before Easter of the previous year the priest had refused to bless the house of the lost woman. And yet Christ had pardoned Mary Magdalene. Perhaps if the priest had blessed the lost woman's house she might have amended her ways. This last reflection presently began to take hold of him to the exclusion of all other thoughts, but on examining it now at this distance of time he perceived that here his instinct had played him false, for at that period he had not yet learnt to know himself. And yet perhaps, even if he had known himself, he would still have gone back on the Saturday to see the lost woman in the lane.

When he turned the corner he saw that Maria Paska was not sitting on her doorstep, but the door was open, a sign that she had no visitor. Involuntarily he imitated the big man and went down the lane in the shadow of the wall, but he wished she had been there on the look-out and that she had risen up with a grave, sad face at his approach. When he reached the end of the lane he saw her drawing water from a well at the side of the house, and his heart gave a jump, for she looked just like the pictures of Mary Magdalene; and she turned and saw him as she was drawing up the bucket, and blushed. Never in his life had he seen a more beautiful woman. Then he was seized with a desire to run away, but he was too shy, and as she re-entered the house carrying the jug of water in her hand she said something to him which he did not understand, but he followed her inside and she shut the door. A little wooden staircase ending in a trapdoor gave access to the upper room, the one with the window over which hung a cross as a protection against temptation, and she led him up, snatching his cap from his head and tossing it aside with a laugh.

Paul went to see her again several times, but after he had been ordained and had taken the vow of chastity he had kept away from all women. His senses seemed to have grown petrified within the frozen armour of his vow, and when he heard scandalous tales of other priests he felt a pride in his own purity, and only thought of his adventure with the woman in the lane as an illness from which he had completely recovered.

During the first years passed in the little village he thought of himself as having already lived his life, as having known all it could offer, misery, humiliation, love, pleasure, sin and expiation; as having withdrawn from the world like some old hermit and waiting only for the Kingdom of God. And now suddenly he beheld the earthly life again in a woman's eyes, and at first he had been so deceived as to mistake it for the life eternal.

To love and be loved, is not this the Kingdom of God upon earth? And his heart swelled within him at the remembrance. O Lord, are we so blind? Where shall we find the light? Paul knew himself to be ignorant: his knowledge was made up of fragments of books of which he only imperfectly understood the meaning, but above all the Bible had impressed him with its romanticism and its realistic pictures of past ages. Wherefore he could place no reliance even on himself nor on his own inward searching: he realized that he had no self-knowledge, that he was not master of himself and that he deceived himself ever and always.

His feet had been set upon the wrong road. He was a man of strong natural instincts, like his forbears, the millers and shepherds, and he suffered because he was not allowed to obey his instincts. Here he got back to his first simple and correct diagnosis of what ailed him: he was unhappy because he was a man and was forbidden to lead man's natural life of love and joy and the fulfilment of life's natural ends. Then he reflected that pleasure enjoyed leaves only horror and anguish behind it; therefore it could not be the flesh that cried out for its chance of life, but rather the soul imprisoned within the flesh that longed to escape from its prison. In those supreme moments of love it had been the soul which had soared upward in a rapid flight, only to fall back more swiftly into its cage; but that instant of freedom had sufficed to show it the place to which it would take its flight when its prison days were ended and the wall of flesh forever overthrown, a place of infinite joy, the Infinite itself.

He smiled at last, saddened and weary. Where had he read all these things? Certainly he must have read them somewhere, for he had no pretensions to evolve new ideas himself. But it was of no consequence, the truth is always the same, alike for all men, as all men's hearts are alike. He had thought himself different from other men, a voluntary exile and worthy of being near to God, and perhaps God was punishing him in this way, by sending him back among men, into the community of passion and of pain.

He must rise up and pursue his appointed way.

He became aware that someone was knocking at the door.

Paul started as though suddenly awakened from sleep and sprang up from his bed with the confused sensation of one who has to depart on a journey and is afraid of being too late. But directly he tried to stand up he was forced to sit down weakly on his bed again, for his limbs gave way under him and he felt as if he had been beaten all over whilst he lay asleep. Crouched together with his head sunk on his breast, he could only nod faintly in response to the knock. His mother had not forgotten to call him early, as he had requested her on the previous day: his mother was following her own straight path, she remembered nothing of what had happened during the night and called him as though this were just like any other morning.

Yes, it was like any other morning. Paul got up again and began to dress, and gradually he pulled himself together and stood stiff and erect in the garments of his order. He flung open the window, and his eyes were dazzled by the vivid light of the silvery sky; the thickets on the hill-side, alive with the song of birds, quivered and sparkled in the morning sun, the wind had dropped and the sound of the church bell vibrated through the pure air.

The bell called him, he lost sight of all external things, although he sought to escape from the things within him: the scent of his room caused him physical distress and the memories it evoked stung him to the quick. The bell went on calling him, but he could not make up his mind to leave his room and he wandered round it almost in a fury. He looked in the mirror and then turned away, but it was useless for him to avoid it; the image of the woman was reflected in his mind as in a mirror, he might break it in a thousand fragments, but each fragment would still retain that image entire and complete.

The second bell for Mass was ringing insistently, inviting him to come: he moved about here and there, searching for something he could not find, and finally sat down at his table and began to write. He began by copying out the verses which said, «Enter ye in by the narrow gate,» etc.; then he crossed them out and on the other side of the paper he wrote: «Please do not expect me again. We have mutually entangled each other in a net of deception and we must cut ourselves loose without delay, if we want to free ourselves and not sink to the bottom. I am coming to you no more; forget me, do not write to me, and do not try to see me again».

Then he went downstairs and called his mother, and held out the letter towards her without looking at her.

"Take this to her at once," he said hoarsely "try and give it into her own hands and then come away immediately."

He felt the letter taken out of his hand and hurried outside, for the moment uplifted and relieved.

Now the bell was ringing the third time, pealing out over the quiet village and the valleys grey in the silvery light of the dawn. Up the hilly road, as though ascending from the depths of the valley, came figures of old men with gnarled sticks hanging from their wrists by leather straps, and women whose heads wrapped in voluminous kerchiefs looked too large for their small bodies. When they had all entered the church and the old men had taken their places in front close by the altar rails, the place was filled with the odour of earth and field, and Antiochus, the youthful sacristan, swung his censer energetically, sending out the smoke in the direction of the old men to drive away the smell. Gradually a dense cloud of incense screened the altar from the rest of the little church, and the brown-faced sacristan in his white surplice and the pale-faced priest in his vestments of red brocade moved about as in a pearly mist. Both Paul and the boy loved the smoke and the scent of the incense and used it lavishly. Turning towards the nave, the priest half closed his eyes and frowned as though the mist impeded his sight; apparently he was displeased at the small number of worshippers and was waiting for others to arrive. And in fact a few late comers did enter then, and last of all his mother, and Paul turned white to the lips.

So the letter had been delivered and the sacrifice was accomplished: a deathlike sweat broke out upon his forehead, and as he raised his hands in consecration his secret prayer was that the offering of his own flesh and blood might be accepted. And he seemed to see the woman reading his letter and falling to the ground in a swoon.

When the Mass was ended he knelt down wearily and recited a Latin prayer in a monotonous voice. The congregation responded, and he felt as though he were dreaming and longed to throw himself down at the foot of the altar and fall asleep like a shepherd on the bare rocks. Dimly through the clouds of incense he saw in her glass-fronted niche the little Madonna which the people believed to be miraculous, a figure as dark and delicate as a cameo in a medallion, and he gazed at it as though he were seeing it again for the first time after a long absence. Where had he been all that time? His thoughts were confused and he could not recollect.

Then suddenly he rose to his feet and turned round and began to address the congregation, a thing he only did very occasionally. He spoke in dialect and in a harsh voice, as though he were scolding the old men, now thrusting their bearded faces between the pillars of the altar rails in order to hear better, and the women crouching on the ground, divided between curiosity and fear. The sacristan, holding the Mass-book in his arms, glanced at Paul out of his long dark eyes, then turned them on the people and shook his head, threatening them in jest if they did not attend.

"Yes," said the priest "the number of you who come here grows ever less; when I have to face you I am almost ashamed, for I feel like a shepherd who has lost his sheep. Only on Sunday is the church a little fuller, but I fear you come because of your scruples and not because of your belief, from habit rather than from need, as you change your clothes or take your rest. Up now, it is time to awake! I do not expect mothers of families, or men who have to be at work before the dawn, to come here every morning, but young women and old men and children, such as I shall see now when I leave the church, standing at their own doors to greet the rising sun, all those should come here to begin the day with God, to praise Him in His own house and to gain strength for the path they have to tread. If you did this the poverty that afflicts you would disappear, and evil habits and temptation would no longer assail you. It is time to awake early in the morning, to wash yourselves and to change your clothing every day and not only on Sundays! So I shall expect you all, beginning from tomorrow, and we will pray together that God will not forsake us and our little village, as He will not forsake the smallest nest, and for those who are sick and cannot come here we will pray that they may recover and be able to march forward too."

He turned round swiftly and the sacristan did the same, and for a few minutes there reigned in the little church a silence so intense that the stone-breaker could be heard at his work behind the ridge. Then a woman got up and approached the priest's mother, placing a hand on her shoulder as she bent down and whispered: "Your son must come at once to hear the confession of King Nicodemus, who is seriously ill."

Roused from her own sad thoughts, the mother raised her eyes to the speaker. She remembered that King Nicodemus was a fantastic old hunter who lived in a hut high up in the mountains, and she asked if Paul would have to climb up there to hear the confession.

"No," whispered the woman "his relations have brought him down to the village."

So the mother went to tell Paul, who was in the little sacristy, disrobing with the help of Antiochus.

"You will come home first and drink your coffee, won't you?" she asked.

He avoided looking at her and did not even answer, but pretended to be in a great hurry to go to the old man who was ill. The thoughts of both mother and son dwelt upon the same thing, the letter which had been delivered to Agnes, but neither spoke of it. Then he hastened away, and she stood there like a block of wood whilst the sacristan busied himself in replacing the vestments in the black cupboard.

"It would have been better if I had not told him about Nicodemus until he had been home and had his coffee," she said.

"A priest must get accustomed to everything," replied Antiochus gravely, poking his head round the cupboard door, and then he added as though to himself as he turned back to his work inside: "Perhaps he is angry with me, because he says I am inattentive: but it's not true, I assure you it's not true! Only when I looked at those old men I felt inclined to laugh, for they did not understand a word of the sermon. They sat there with their mouths open, but they understood nothing. I bet you that old Marco Panizza really thinks he ought to wash his face every day, he who never washes at all except at Easter and Christmas! And you'll see that from now on they will all come to church every day, because he told them that poverty would disappear if they did that".

The mother still stood there, her hands clasped beneath her apron.

"The poverty of the soul" she said, to show that she at least had understood. But Antiochus only looked at her as he had looked at the old men, with a strong desire to laugh. Because he was quite sure that nobody could understand these matters as he understood them, he who already knew the four gospels by heart and intended to be a priest himself, which fact did not prevent him from being as mischievous and inquisitive as other boys.

As soon as he had finished putting everything in order and the priest's mother had gone away, Antiochus locked the sacristy and walked across the little garden attached to the church, all overgrown with rosemary and as deserted as a cemetery. But instead of going home to where his mother kept a tavern in one corner of the village square, he ran off to the presbytery to hear the latest news of King Nicodemus, and also for another reason.

"Your son scolded me for not paying attention" he repeated uneasily, whilst the priest's mother was busy preparing her Paul's breakfast. "Perhaps he won't have me as sacristan any longer, perhaps he will take Ilario Panizza. But Ilario cannot read, whereas I have even learnt to read Latin. Besides, Ilario is so dirty. What do you think? Will he send me away?"

"He wants you to pay attention, that is all: it is not right to laugh in church" she answered sternly and gravely.

"He is very angry. Perhaps he did not sleep last night, on account of the wind. Did you hear what an awful wind?"

The woman made no reply; she went into the dining-room and placed on the table enough bread and biscuits to satisfy the twelve apostles. Probably Paul would not touch a thing, but the mere act of moving about and making preparations for him, as though he were sure to come in as merry and hungry as a mountain shepherd, did something to assuage her trouble and perhaps quiet her conscience, which every moment stung her more and more sharply, and the boy's very remark, that "perhaps he was angry because he did not sleep last night," only increased her uneasiness. Her heavy footsteps echoed through the silent rooms as she went to and fro: she felt instinctively that although apparently *all was over*, in reality it was all only just beginning. She had well understood the words he spoke from the altar, that one must awake early and wash oneself and march forward, and she went to and fro, up and down, trying to imagine that she was marching forward in very truth. She went upstairs to put his room in order; but the mirror and the perfumes still vexed and alarmed her, in spite of the assurance that everything was now at an end, while a vision of Paul, pale and rigid as a corpse, seemed to meet her eyes from the depths of that cursed mirror, to hang with his cassock on the wall and lie stretched lifeless upon the bed. And her heart was heavy within her, as though some inward paralysis prevented her breathing.

The pillow-slip was still damp with Paul's tears and his fevered anguish of the night, and as she drew it off to replace it with a fresh one the thought came to her, for the first time in her life: "But why are priests forbidden to marry?".

And she thought of Agnes's wealth, and how she owned a large house with gardens and orchards and fields.

Then suddenly she felt horribly guilty in even entertaining such thoughts, and quickly drawing on the fresh pillow-slip she went away into her own room.

Marching forward? Yes, she had been marching since dawn and was yet only at the beginning of the way. And however far one went, one always came back to the same place. She went downstairs and sat by the fire beside Antiochus, who had not moved and was determined to wait there all day, if needs be, for the sake of seeing his superior and making his peace with him. He sat very still, one leg crossed over the other and his hands clasped round his knee, and presently he remarked, not without a slight accent of reproach: "You ought to have taken him his coffee into the church, as you do when he is delayed there hearing the women's confessions. As it is, he will be famished!"

"And how was I to know he would be sent for in such a hurry? The old man is dying, it seems" retorted the mother.

"I don't think that can be true. His grandchildren want him to die because he has some money to leave. I know the old chap! I saw him once when I went up into the mountains with my father: he was sitting amongst the rocks in the sun, with a dog and a tame eagle beside him and all sorts of dead animals all round. That is not how God orders us to live!"

"What does He order, then?"

"He orders us to live amongst men, to cultivate the ground, and not to hide our money, but to give it to the poor."

The little sacristan spoke with a man's confidence, and the priest's mother was touched and smiled. After all, if Antiochus could say such sensible things it was because he had been taught by her Paul. It was her Paul who taught them all to be good, wise and prudent; and when he really wished to he succeeded in convincing even old men whose opinions were already fixed, and even thoughtless children. She sighed, and bending down to draw the coffee-pot nearer the glowing embers, she said: "You talk like a little saint, Antiochus; but it remains to be seen if you will do as you say when you're a man, whether you really will give your money to the poor".

"Yes, I shall give everything to the poor. I shall have a great deal of money, because my mother makes a lot with her tavern, and my father is a forest keeper and earns pretty well, too. I shall give all I get to the poor: God tells us to do that, and He Himself will provide for us. And the Bible says, the ravens do not sow, neither do they reap, yet they have their food from God, and the lily of the valley is clothed more splendidly than the king."

"Yes, Antiochus, when a man is alone he can do that, but what if he has children?"

"That makes no difference. Besides, I shall never have children; priests are not allowed to have any."

She turned to look at him; his profile was towards her, against the bright background of the open doorway and the courtyard outside; it was a profile of pure, firm outline and dark skin, almost like a head of bronze, with long lashes shading the eyes with their large dark pupils. And as she gazed at the boy she could have wept, but she knew not why.

"Are you quite sure you want to be a priest?" she asked.

"Yes, if that is God's will."

"Priests are not allowed to marry, and suppose that some day you wanted to take a wife?"

"I shall not want a wife, since God has forbidden it."

"God? But it is the Pope who has forbidden it" said the mother, somewhat taken aback at the boy's answer.

"The Pope is God's representative on earth."

"But in olden times priests had wives and families, just as the Protestant clergy have now" she urged.

"That is a different thing," said the boy, growing warm over the argument; "*we* ought not to have them!"

"The priests in olden times..." she persisted.

But the sacristan was well-informed. "Yes, the priests in olden times," he said "but then they themselves held a meeting and decided against it; and those who had no wives or families, the younger ones, were the very ones who opposed marriage the most strongly. That is as it should be."

"The younger ones!" repeated the mother as if to herself. "But they know nothing about it! And then they may repent, they may even go astray," she added in a low voice "they may come to reason and argue like the old priest."

A tremor seized her and she looked swiftly round to assure herself that the ghost was not there, instantly repenting for having thus evoked it. She did not wish even to think about it, and least of all in connexion with *that matter.* Was it not all ended? Moreover, Antiochus's face wore an expression of the deepest scorn.

"That man was not a priest, he was the devil's brother come to earth! God save us from him! We had best not even think about him!" and he made the sign of the cross. Then he continued, with recovered serenity: "As for repenting! Do you suppose that *he,* your son, ever dreams of repenting?".

It hurt her to hear the boy talk like that. She longed to be able to tell him something of her trouble, to warn him for the future, yet at the same time she rejoiced at his words, as though the conscience of the innocent lad were speaking to her conscience to commend and encourage it.

"Does he, does my Paul say it is right for priests not to marry?" she asked in a low voice.

"If *he* does not say it is right, who should say so? Of course he says it is right; hasn't he said so to you? A fine thing it would be to see a priest with his wife beside him and a child in his arms! And when he ought to go and say Mass he has to nurse the baby because it's howling! What a joke! Imagine your son with one child in his arms and another hanging on to his cassock!"

The mother smiled wanly; but there passed before her eyes a fleeting vision of lovely children running about the house, and there was a pang at her heart. Antiochus laughed aloud, his dark eyes and white teeth flashing in his brown face, but there was something cruel in his laughter.

"A priest's wife would be a funny thing! When they went out for a walk together they would look from behind like two women! And would she go and confess to him, if they lived in a place where there was no other priest?"

"What does a mother do? Who do I confess to?"

"A mother is different. And who is there that your son could marry? The granddaughter of King Nicodemus, perhaps?"

He began to laugh merrily again, for the granddaughter of King Nicodemus was the most unfortunate girl in the village, a cripple and an idiot. But he instantly grew serious again when the mother, forced to speak by a will other than her own, said softly: "For that matter, there is someone, Agnes".

But Antiochus objected jealously: "She is ugly, I don't like her, and he does not like her either".

Then the mother began to praise Agnes, but she spoke almost in a whisper as though afraid of being overheard by anyone except the boy, while Antiochus, his hands still clasped round his knee, shook his head energetically, his lower lip stuck out in disgust like a ripe cherry.

"No, no, I don't like her! Can't you hear what I say? She is ugly and proud and old. And besides..."

A step sounded in the little hall and instantly they both were silent and stood waiting.

Paul sat down at the table, which was laid ready for breakfast, and put his hat on the chair beside him, and while his mother was pouring out his coffee he asked in a calm voice: "Did you take that letter?".

She nodded, pointing towards the kitchen for fear the boy should hear.

"Who is there?" asked Paul.

"Antiochus."

"Antiochus!" he called, and with one spring the boy was before him, cap in hand, standing to attention like a little soldier.

"Listen, Antiochus, you must go back to the church and get everything ready for taking extreme unction to the old man later on."

The boy was speechless with joy: so *he* was no longer angry and was not going to dismiss him and take another boy in his place!

"Wait a moment, have you had anything to eat?"

"He would not have anything to eat, he never will" said the mother.

"Sit down there," ordered Paul "you must eat. Mother, give him something."

It was not the first time that Antiochus had sat at the priest's table, so he obeyed without shyness, though his heart beat fast. He was aware somehow that his position had changed, that the priest was speaking to him in a way different from usual; he could not explain how or why, he only felt there was a difference. He looked up in Paul's face as though he saw him for the first time, with mingled fear and joy. Fear and joy and a whole throng of new emotions, gratitude, hope and pride, filled his heart as a nest full of warm fledglings ready to spread their wings and fly away.

"Then at two o'clock you must come for your lesson. It is time to set to work seriously with Latin; and I must write for a new grammar, mine is centuries old."

Antiochus had stopped eating: now he went very red and offered his services enthusiastically without inquiring the why or the wherefore. The priest looked at him with a smile, then turned his face to the window, through which the trees could be seen waving against the clear sky, and his thoughts were evidently far away. Antiochus felt again as if he had been dismissed and his spirits fell; he brushed the crumbs from the tablecloth, folded his napkin carefully and carried the cups into the kitchen. He prepared to wash up, too, and would have done it very well, for he was accustomed to washing glasses in his mother's wine-shop; but the priest's mother would not allow it.

"Go to the church and get ready" she whispered, pushing him away. He went out immediately, but before going to the church he ran round to his mother to warn her to have the house clean and tidy as the priest was coming to see her.

Meanwhile the priest's mother had gone back into the dining-room, where Paul was still idling at the table with a newspaper in front of him. Usually, when he was at home, he sat in his own room, but this morning he was afraid of going up there again. He sat reading the newspaper, but his thoughts were elsewhere. He was thinking of the old dying hunter, who had once confessed to him that he shunned the company of men because «they are evil itself» and men in mockery had called him King, as they had called Christ King of the Jews. But Paul was not interested in the old man's confession; his thoughts turned rather to Antiochus and his father and mother, for he meant to ask the latter whether they conscientiously realized what they were doing in allowing the boy to have his own way and carry out his unreasoning fancy for becoming a priest. But even this was really of little importance: what Paul actually wanted was to get away from his own thoughts, and when his mother came into the room he bowed his head over his paper, for he knew that she alone could divine what those thoughts were.

He sat there with bowed head, but he forbade his lips to frame the question he longed to ask. The letter had been delivered; what more was there for him to know? The stone of the sepulchre had been rolled into its place: but ah! how it weighed upon him, how alive he felt, buried alive beneath that great stone!

His mother began to clear the table, putting each object back in the cupboard that served as a sideboard. It was so quiet that the birds could be heard chirping in the bushes and the regular tap-tap of the stone-breaker by the roadside. It seemed like the end of the world, as though the last habitation of living men was this little white room, with its time-blackened furniture and its tiled flooring, upon which the green and gold light from the high window cast a tremulous reflection as of water and made the small place seem like some prison chamber in the dungeon of a castle.

Paul had drunk his coffee and eaten his biscuits as usual, and now he was reading the news of the great world far away. Outwardly there was nothing to show that this day was in any way different from other days, but his mother would rather he had gone up to his room as was his custom and shut the door. And why, since he was sitting there, did he not ask her more about her errand, and to whom she had given the letter? She went to the kitchen door with a cup in her hand, then carried it back to the table and stood there.

"Paul," she said "I gave the letter into her own hand. She was already up and dressed, and in the garden."

"Very well" he answered, without raising his eyes from the newspaper.

But she could not leave him, she felt she must speak; something stronger than her will impelled her, something stronger even than the will of her son. She cleared her throat and fixed her eyes on the little Japanese landscape painted at the bottom of the cup she was holding, its colours stained and darkened with coffee. Then she went on with her tale: "She was in the garden, for she gets up early. I went straight to her and gave her the letter: nobody saw. She took it and looked at it; then she looked at me, but still she did not open it. I said «There is no answer» and turned to go away, but she said «Wait». Then she opened the letter as if to show me there was no secret in it, and she turned as white as the paper itself. Then she said to me «Go, and God be with you!»".

"That's enough!" he cried sharply, still without looking up, but his mother saw the lashes quiver over his downcast eyes and his face turn as white as that of Agnes. For a moment she thought he was about to faint, then the blood slowly came back into his face and she breathed again with relief. Such moments as these were terrible, but they must be met bravely and overcome. She opened her lips to say something else, to murmur at least, "See what you have done, how you have hurt both yourself and her!" but at that instant he looked up, jerking his head back as though to drive the blood of evil passion from his face, and glaring angrily at his mother, he said roughly: "Now that is enough! Do you hear? It's enough! I absolutely refuse to hear another word on this matter, otherwise I shall do what you threatened to do last night: I shall go away".

Then he got up quickly, but instead of going to his room he left the house again. His mother went into the kitchen, the cup still in her trembling hands; she put it down on the table and leaned against the corner of the fireplace, utterly broken down. She knew now he had gone away forever; even if he came back he would no longer be her Paul, but a poor wretch possessed by his evil passion, one who looked with threatening eyes at whoever crossed his path, like some thief lying in wait to commit a crime.

And Paul, indeed, was like one who has fled from home in fear. He had rushed out to avoid going up to his room, for he had an idea that Agnes might have got in secretly and be waiting for him there, with her white face and the letter in her hand. He had escaped from the house in order to escape from himself, but he was carried away by his passion more violently than by the wind on the night before. He crossed the meadow without any definite aim, feeling as though he were some inanimate thing flung bodily against the wall of Agnes's house and thrown back by the rebound as far as the square before the church, where the old men and the boys and the beggars sit on the low parapet all day long. Scarce knowing how he had come there, Paul stayed a little while talking to one or another of them without heeding their replies, and then descended the steep road that led from the village down to the valley. But he saw nothing of the road he trod nor the landscape before his eyes: his whole world had turned upside-down and was a mere chaos of rocks and ruins, upon which he looked down as boys lie flat on the ground at the cliff's edge to gaze over into the depths below.

He turned and climbed up again towards the church. The village seemed almost deserted; here and there a peach tree showed its ripe fruit over a garden wall and little white clouds floated across the clear September sky like a peaceful flock of sheep. In one house a child was crying, from another came the regular sound of the weaver at his loom. The rural *guardia*, half-keeper, half-police, who had charge of the village also, the only public functionary in the place, came strolling along the road with his great dog on a leash. He wore a mixed costume, the hunter's jacket of discoloured velvet with the blue, red-striped trousers of his official uniform, and his dog was a huge black and red animal with bloodshot eyes, something between a lion and a wolf, known and feared by villagers and peasants, by shepherds and hunters, by thieves and children alike. The keeper kept his beast beside him day and night, chiefly for fear of him being poisoned. The dog growled when he saw the priest, but at a sign from his master he was quiet and hung his head.

The keeper stopped in front of the priest and gave a military salute, then said solemnly: "I went early this morning to see the sick man. His temperature is forty, his pulse a hundred and two. In my poor opinion he has inflammation of the loins, and his granddaughter wanted me to give him quinine". (The keeper had charge of the drugs and medicines supplied for the parish and permitted himself to go round visiting the sick, which was exceeding his duty, but gave him importance in his own eyes, as he imagined he was thus taking the place of the doctor who only came to the village twice a week.) "But I said, «Gently, my girl; in my humble opinion he does not want quinine, but another sort of medicine». The girl began to cry, but she shed no tears; may I die if I judged wrongly! She wanted me to rush off immediately to call the doctor, but I said, «The doctor is coming tomorrow, Sunday, but if you are in such a hurry then send a man yourself to fetch him! The sick man can well afford to pay a doctor to see him die, he has spent no money during his life», I was quite right, wasn't I?".

The keeper waited gravely for the priest's approval, but Paul was looking at the dog, now quiet and docile at his master's bidding, and he was thinking to himself:

"If we could only thus keep our passions on a leash!" And then he said aloud, but in an absent-minded way, "Oh yes, he can wait till the doctor comes tomorrow. But he is seriously ill, all the same."

"Well then, if he is seriously ill," persisted the keeper firmly and not without contempt for the priest's apparent indifference "a man had better go for the doctor at once. The old fellow can pay, he is not a pauper. But his granddaughter disobeyed my orders and did not give him the medicine I myself prepared and left for him."

"He should receive the Communion first of all" said Paul.

"But you have told me that a sick person may receive the Communion even if they are not fasting?"

"Well then," said the priest, losing patience at last, "the old man did not want the medicine; he clenched his teeth, and he has them all still sound, and struck out as if nothing was the matter with him."

"And then the granddaughter, in my humble opinion," continued the keeper indignantly "has no right to order me, an official, to rush off for the doctor as though I were a servant! It was not a question of an accident or anything requiring the doctor's official presence, and I have other things to do. I must now go down to the river by the ford, because I have received information that some benefactor of his neighbours has placed dynamite in the water to destroy the trout. My respects!"

He repeated the military salute and departed, jerking his dog up by the leash. Suddenly sharing its master's repressed contempt, the animal stalked off waving its ferocious tail; it did not growl at the priest, but merely turned its head to give him a parting glance of menace out of its savage eyes.

Having completed his preparations for carrying extreme unction to the old man, Antiochus was leaning over the parapet of the piazza under the shade of the elms, waiting for the priest; and when he saw him approaching, the boy darted into the sacristy and waited with the surplice in his hands. The pair were ready in a few minutes, Paul in surplice and stole, carrying the silver amphora of oil, Antiochus robed in red from head to foot and holding a brocade umbrella with gold fringe open over Paul's head, so that he and his silver amphora were in shadow whilst the boy himself appeared the more brilliant in the sunshine in contrast to the black and white figure of the priest. Antiochus's face wore a look of almost tragic gravity, for he was much impressed with his own importance and imagined himself specially deputed to protect the holy oil. Nevertheless this did not prevent him from grinning with amusement at the sight of the old men hurriedly shuffling down from the parapet as the little procession passed, and the boys kneeling with their faces to the wall instead of towards the priest. The youngsters jumped up immediately, however, and followed Antiochus, who rang his bell before each door to warn the people; dogs barked, the weavers stopped their looms and the women thrust their heads out of the windows to see, and the whole village was in a tremor of mysterious excitement.

A woman who was coming from the fountain bearing a jug of water on her head set down her jug upon the ground and knelt beside it. And the priest grew pale, for he recognized one of Agnes's servants, and a nameless dread seized upon him, so that unconsciously he clasped the silver amphora tightly between his hands as though seeking support there.

The attendant crowd of boys grew larger as they approached the old hunter's dwelling. This was a two-story cottage built of rough stone and standing a little back from the road on the side towards the valley; it had a single unglazed window and in front a small yard of bare earth enclosed by a low wall. The door stood open and the priest knew that the old man was lying fully dressed on a mat in the lower room; so he entered at once, reciting the prayers for the sick, whilst Antiochus closed the umbrella and rang his bell loudly to drive away the children as if they were flies. But the room was empty and the mat unoccupied; perhaps the old man had at last consented to go to bed or had been carried there in a dying condition. The priest pushed open the door of an inner room, but that too was empty; so, puzzled, he returned to the door, whence he saw the old man's granddaughter limping down the road with a bottle in her hand. She had been to fetch the medicine.

"Where is your grandfather?" asked Paul, as the girl crossed herself on entering the house. She glanced at the empty mat and gave a scream, and the inquisitive boys immediately swarmed over the wall and round the door, engaging in a free fight with Antiochus, who tried to oppose their entrance, till Paul himself sternly bade them disperse.

"Where is he? Where is he?" cried the granddaughter, running from room to room, whereupon one of the boys, the last to join the crowd, sauntered up with his hands in his pockets and inquired casually, "Are you looking for the King? He went down there."

"Down where?"

"Down there" repeated the boy, pointing with his nose towards the valley.

The girl rushed down the steep path and the boys after her: the priest signed to Antiochus to reopen the umbrella and gravely and in silence the two returned to the church, whilst the villagers gathered together in wondering groups and the news of the sick man's flight spread from mouth to mouth.

Paul was back again in his quiet dining-room, seated at the table and waited on by his mother. Fortunately there was now something they dare talk about and the flight of King Nicodemus was being discussed. Having hastily deposited the silver amphora and other things taken out for the rite and doffed his red cope, Antiochus had run off to collect news. The first time he came back it was with a strange report; the old man had disappeared and his relations were said to have carried him off in order to get possession of his money.

"They say that his dog and his eagle came down and carried him off themselves!" corrected some sceptic jestingly.

"I don't believe in the dog," said one of the old men "but the eagle is no joke. I remember that when I was a boy, one carried off a heavy sheep from our yard."

Then Antiochus came back with the further news that the sick man had been overtaken halfway up to the mountain plateau, where he wished to die. The last upflickering of his fever lent him a fictitious strength and the dying hunter walked like a somnambulist to the place where he longed to be, and in order not to worry him and make him worse, his relatives had accompanied him and seen him safely to his own hut.

"Now sit down and eat" said the priest to the boy.

Antiochus obeyed and took his place at the table, but not without first glancing inquiringly at the priest's mother. She smiled and signed to him to do as he was bidden and the boy felt that he had become one of the family. He could not know, innocent child, that the other two, having exhausted the subject of the old hunter, were afraid of being alone together. The mother would see her son's uneasy wandering eyes arrested suddenly, as though upon some unseen object, with a stony, sombre gaze, overshadowed by the darkness of his mind, and he in turn would start from his preoccupation, aware that she was observing him and divining his inward grief. But when she had placed the meal on the table she left the room and did not return.

With the bright noonday the wind rose again, but now it was a soft west wind that scarcely stirred the trees upon the ridge; the room was flooded with sunshine chequered by the dancing of the leaves outside the window, and white clouds drifted across the sky like harp-strings whereon the wind played its gentle music.

The charm was broken suddenly by a knock at the door and Antiochus ran to open. A pale young widow with frightened eyes stood on the threshold and asked to see the priest. By the hand she held fast a little girl, with small, livid face and a red scarf tied over her untidy black hair; and, as the child dragged and struggled from side to side in her efforts to free herself, her eyes blazed like a wild cat's. "She is ill," said the widow "and I want the priest to read the gospel over her to drive out the evil spirit that has taken possession of her."

Puzzled and scared, Antiochus stood holding the door half open: this was not the time to worry the priest with such matters, and moreover the girl, who was twisting herself all to one side and trying to bite her mother's hand as she could not escape, was truly an object of both fear and pity.

"She is possessed, you see" said the widow, turning red with shame. So then Antiochus let her in immediately and even helped her to push in the child, who clung to the jamb of the door and resisted with all her might.

On hearing what was the matter and that this was already the third day on which the little victim had behaved so strangely, always trying to escape, deaf and dumb to all persuasions, the priest had her brought in to him, and taking her by the shoulders he examined her eyes and her mouth.

"Has she been much in the sun?" he inquired.

"It's not that" whispered the mother. "I think she is possessed by an evil spirit. No," she added, sobbing, "my little girl is no longer alone!"

Paul rose to fetch his Testament from his room, then stopped and sent Antiochus for it. The book was placed open on the table, and with his hand upon the burning head of the child, clasped tightly in the arms of her kneeling mother, he read aloud: "And they arrived at the country of the Gadarenes, which is over against Galilee. And when he went forth to land, there met him out of the city a certain man which had devils a long time, and wear no clothes, neither abode in any house, but in the tombs. When he saw Jesus he cried out and fell down before him, and with a loud voice said, «What have I to do with thee, Jesus, thou Son of God most high? I beseech thee, torment me not»".

Antiochus turned over the page of the book and his eyes strayed to the priest's hand which rested on the table; at the words "What have I to do with thee" he saw the hand tremble, and looking up quickly he perceived that Paul's eyes were full of tears. Then, overcome by an irresistible emotion, the boy knelt down beside the widow, but still keeping his arm stretched out to touch the book. And he thought to himself: "Surely *he* is the best man in all the world, for he weeps when he reads the word of God!". And he did not venture to raise his eyes again to look at Paul, but with his free hand he pulled the little girl's skirt to keep her quiet, though not without a secret fear that the demons who were being exorcised from her body would enter into his own.

The possessed child had ceased throwing herself about and stood up straight and stiff, her thin brown neck stretched to its full length, her little chin stuck forward over the knot of her kerchief and her eyes fixed upon the priest's face. Gradually her expression changed, her mouth relaxed and opened, and it seemed as if the words of the Gospel, the murmuring of the wind and the rustle of the trees on the ridge were working upon her as a charm. Suddenly she tore her skirt from Antiochus's restraining hand and fell on her knees beside him, and the priest's hand which had rested upon her head remained outstretched above it, as his tremulous voice continued reading: "Now the man out of whom the devils were departed besought him that he might be with him: but Jesus sent him away, saying, Return to thine own house and show how great things God hath done unto thee...".

He ceased reading and withdrew his hand. The child was now perfectly quiet and had turned her face wonderingly towards the boy, and in the silence that succeeded the Gospel words nothing was audible save the trees rustling in the breeze and the faint tap-tap of the stone-breaker by the roadside.

Paul was suffering acutely. Not for one moment had he shared the widow's superstition that the girl was possessed by a devil and he felt, therefore, that he had been reading the Gospel without belief. The only devil which existed was the one within himself, and this one would not be driven forth. And yet there had been a moment when he had felt nearer to God: «What have I to do with thee?». And it seemed to him that those three believers in front of him, and his own mother kneeling at the kitchen door, were bowed, not before his power, but before his utter wretchedness. Yet when the widow bent low to kiss his feet he drew back sharply: he thought of his mother, *who knew all*, and feared lest she should misjudge him.

The widow was so overwhelmed with mortification when she raised her head that the two children began to laugh, and even Paul's distress relaxed a little.

"That's all right, get up now," he said "the child is quiet."

They all rose to their feet and Antiochus ran to open the door, at which now somebody else was knocking. It was the keeper with his dog on the leash, and Antiochus burst out instantly, his face beaming with joy: "A miracle has just happened! He has driven out the devils from the body of Nina Masia!".

But the keeper did not believe in miracles; he stood a little away from the door and said: "Then let us make room for them to escape!".

"They will enter into the body of your dog" cried Antiochus.

"They cannot enter because they are there already" replied the keeper. He spoke in jest, but maintained his usual gravity. On the threshold of the room he drew himself up and saluted the priest without condescending even to glance at the women.

"Can I speak to you in private, sir?"

The women withdrew into the kitchen and Antiochus carried the Testament upstairs. When he came down, although still full of excitement at the miracle, he stopped to listen to what the keeper was saying: "I beg your pardon for bringing this animal into the house, but he is quite clean and he will give no trouble because he understands where he is." (The dog, in fact, was standing motionless, with lowered eyes and hanging tail.) "I've come about the matter of old Nicodemus Pania, nicknamed King Nicodemus. He is back in his hut and has expressed the wish to see you again and to receive extreme unction. In my humble opinion...".

"Good heavens!" exclaimed the priest impatiently, but the next instant he was filled with childish joy at the thought of going up to the mountain plateau and by physical exertion banishing for a time the perplexities that tormented him.

"Yes, yes," he added quickly "and I shall want a horse. What is the road like?"

"I will see about the horse and the road," said the keeper "that is my duty."

The priest offered him a drink. On principle the keeper never accepted anything from anyone, not even a glass of wine, but on this occasion he felt that his own civil functions and the priest's religious functions were so much each a part of the other that he accepted the invitation; so he drank, and emptied the last drops of wine on the ground (since the earth claims her share of whatever man consumes), and expressed his thanks with a military salute. Then the great dog wagged his tail and looked up at Paul with an offer of friendship in his eyes.

Antiochus was ready to open the door again and then returned to the dining-room to await orders. He was sorry for his mother, waiting in vain for the priest in the little room behind the bar, which had been specially cleaned up for the occasion and the tray with glasses placed ready for the guest; but duty before all things and the visit would obviously be impossible that day.

"What must I prepare?" he asked, imitating the keeper's solemn tones. "Shall we take the umbrella?"

"What are you thinking of! I am going on horseback and you need not come at all. I could take you up behind me, however."

"No, I will walk, I am never tired," urged the boy, and in a few minutes he was ready, with a little box in his hand and his red cope folded over his arm. As far as he was concerned, he would have liked to take the umbrella too, but he was obliged to obey superior orders.

Whilst he was waiting for the priest in front of the church all the ragged urchins who made of the square their regular playground and battlefield gathered round him curiously without venturing too near, and regarded the box with respect not unmixed with terror.

"Let's go nearer" said one.

"You keep your distance, or I'll let loose the keeper's dog at you!" shouted Antiochus.

"The keeper's dog? Why, you daren't go within ten miles of him!" jeered the urchins.

"Daren't I?" said Antiochus with magnificent scorn.

"No, you daren't! And you think you're as good as the Lord Himself because you're carrying the holy oil!"

"If I were you," advised one open-minded youth "I should make off with that box and perform all kinds of sorceries with the holy oil."

"Be off, you horse-fly! The devil that came out of Nina Masia's body has entered into yours!"

"What's that? The devil?" cried the boys in chorus.

"Yes," said Antiochus solemnly "this very afternoon *he* drove out a devil from the body of Nina Masia. Here she comes."

The widow, leading the little girl by the hand, was just coming out of the presbytery; the boys all rushed to meet her and in one moment the news of the miracle spread through the village. Then occurred a scene which recalled that which had taken place on the first arrival of the priest. The whole population assembled together in the square and Nina Masia was placed by her mother on the top step before the church door, where she sat, thin and brown-skinned, with her green eyes and the red kerchief over her head, looking like some primitive idol set up to be worshipped by those simple and credulous country folk.

The women began to weep and all wanted to touch the girl. Meanwhile the keeper had arrived on the scene with his dog, and then the priest crossed the square on horseback. The crowd immediately collected around him and made a procession to follow him, but whilst he waved his hand to them and turned from side to side acknowledging their greetings, his annoyance at what had happened was even greater than his distress. When he reached the top of the hill he reined in his horse and seemed about to speak, then suddenly put spurs to the animal and rode rapidly down the road. He had a desperate craving to gallop furiously away, to escape through the valley and lose himself and his whole being somewhere in that wide horizon spread out before his gaze.

The wind was freshening: the afternoon sun shone warmly on the thickets and bushes, the river reflected the blue sky and the spray thrown up by the mill-wheel sparkled like diamonds. The keeper with his dog and Antiochus with his box descended the hill soberly, fully conscious of their office, and presently Paul drew rein and rode along quietly. After crossing the river the road became a mere path and wound upwards towards the plateau, bordered by stones and low walls, rocks and stunted trees, and the west wind blew sweet and warm, heavy-laden with perfume, as though it had gathered all the thyme flowers and wild roses it had found upon its way and was now strewing them again upon the earth.

The path wound ever upwards: when they turned round the side of the hill and lost sight of the village, the world seemed nothing but wind and stones, and white vapours that on the horizon linked earth and sky in one. From time to time the dog barked, and the echo in the hills seemed to bring him answers from other dogs all around.

When they were half-way to their destination the priest offered to take Antiochus up behind him on the horse, but the boy refused, and only very unwillingly yielded up the box. And only then did he permit himself to open a conversation with the keeper; a vain attempt, however, for the keeper never forgot his own imaginary importance for one moment. Every now and then he would stop, with a portentous frown, and drawing the peak of his cap low over his eyes he would inspect the landscape on every side, as though the whole world belonged to him and were threatened with some imminent peril. Then the dog would stop too, rigid on his four paws, snuffing the wind and quivering from ears to tail. Luckily all was serene on that windy afternoon, the only moving things in sight being the agile goats climbing on distant rocks, black silhouettes against the blue sky and rosy clouds.

At last they came to a sort of declivity covered with masses of granite, a regular waterfall of rocks balanced one upon another with marvellous precision. Antiochus recognized the place, as he had once been there with his father, and whilst the priest kept to the path, which wound some considerable way round, and the keeper followed him as in duty bound, the boy scrambled down from rock to rock and was the first to reach the hut of the old hunter.

The hut was a ramshackle erection of logs and boughs surrounded by a partly natural enclosure of great boulders, against which the old man, in order to complete this sort of prehistoric fortress, had piled other stones in large numbers. The sun slanted down into this enclosure as into a well: the view was completely shut in on three sides, and only on the right, between two rocks, a silver streak in the blue distance, might be discerned the sea.

On hearing steps the old man's grandson thrust his curly black head out of the hut door.

"They are coming" announced Antiochus.

"Who are coming?"

"The priest and the keeper."

The man sprang out, as agile and hairy as his own goats, and swore roundly at the keeper for always interfering in other people's business.

"I'll break all his bones for him!" he growled threateningly, but when he saw the dog he drew back, while the old man's dog ran forward to sniff at and greet the visitor.

Antiochus took charge of the box again and sat down on a stone facing the opening in the rocks. All around were an immense number of wild-boar-skins, striped black and grey, and of marten skins flecked with gold, spread out on the rocks to dry. Inside the hut he could see the form of the old man lying on a heap of other skins, his dark face, framed in the white hair and beard, already set in the composure of approaching death. The priest was bending down to interrogate him, but the dying man made no reply, and lay with closed eyes and a drop of blood trembling on his violet lips. A little way off, on another stone, sat the keeper with his dog stretched at his feet and his eyes also fixed on the interior of the hut. He was indignant because the dying man was disobeying the law in not declaring what was his last will and testament, and as Antiochus turned his mischievous eyes in that direction he thought somewhat maliciously that the keeper would have liked to set his dog on the stubborn old hunter as on a thief.

Inside the hut the priest bent still lower, his hands clasped between his knees, his face heavy with weariness and displeasure. He too was silent now: he almost seemed to have forgotten why he was there and sat listening to the wind as if it were the distant murmur of the sea. Suddenly the keeper's dog sprang up barking, and Antiochus heard the rustle of wings over his head: he looked up and saw the old hunter's tame eagle alighting on a rock, with its great wings outspread and slowly beating the air like an immense black fan.

Inside the hut Paul was thinking to himself: "And this is death. This man fled from other men because he was afraid of committing murder or some other great crime. And here he lies now, a stone amongst stones. So shall I lie in thirty, forty years, after an exile that has lasted through eternity. And perhaps she will still be expecting me tonight...".

He started up. Ah, no, he was not dead as he had thought: life was beating within him, surging up strong and tenacious like the eagle amongst the stones.

"I must remain up here all night" he told himself. "If I can get through this night without seeing her I shall be saved."

He went outside and sat down beside Antiochus. The sun was sinking in a crimson sky, the shadows of the high rocks were lengthening over the enclosure and the wind-tossed bushes, and in the same way as he could not distinguish objects clearly in the uncertain light without, so Paul could not tell which of the two desires within him was the strongest. Presently he said: "The old man cannot speak now, he is dying. It is time to administer extreme unction, and if he dies we must arrange for the body to be moved. It will be necessary..." he added as though to himself, but did not dare to complete the sentence, "it will be necessary to spend the night here".

Antiochus got up and began to make preparations for the ceremony. He opened the box, pressing the silver fasteners with enjoyment, and drew out the white cloth and the amphora of oil: then he unfolded his red cope and put it on... He might have been himself the priest! When everything was ready they went back into the hut, where the grandson, on his knees, was supporting the dying man's head. Antiochus knelt down on the other side, with the folds of his cope spread out on the ground. He laid the white cloth over the stone that served as a table, and the scarlet of his cope was reflected in the silver amphora. The keeper, too, knelt down outside the hut, with his dog beside him.

Then the priest anointed the old man's forehead, and the palms of his hands which had never sought to do violence to anyone, and his feet which had borne him far from men as from evil itself.

The setting sun shone direct into the hut with a last dazzling splendour, lighting up Antiochus in his scarlet cope, so that between the old man and the priest he looked like a live coal amongst dead cinders.

"I shall have to go back" thought Paul. "I have no excuse for remaining here." Presently he went outside the hut and said: "There is no hope, he is quite unconscious."

"Comatose" said the keeper with precision.

"He cannot live more than a few hours and arrangements must be made for transporting the body down to the village" continued Paul; and he longed to add "And I must stay here all night" but he was ashamed of his untruth.

Moreover he was beginning now to feel the need of walking and a craving to get back to the village. As night fell the thought of sin began subtly to attract him again and drew him in with the invisible net of darkness. He felt it and was afraid; but he kept guard over himself, and he knew his conscience was awake and ready to uphold him.

"If only I could get through this one night without seeing her I should be saved!" was his silent cry. If only someone would detain him by force! If the old man would revive and hold him fast by the hem of his robe!

He sat down again and cast about for some excuse for delaying his departure. The sun had now sunk below the edge of the high plateau, and the trunks of the oaks stood out boldly against the red glow of the sky like the pillars of some gigantic portico, surmounted by an immense black roof. Not even the presence of death could mar the peace of that majestic solitude. Paul was weary and, as in the morning at the foot of the altar, he would have liked to lie down upon the stones and fall asleep.

Meanwhile the keeper had come to a decision on his own account. He entered the hut and, kneeling down beside the dying man, whispered something into his ear. The grandson looked on with suspicion and contempt, then approached the priest and said: "Now that you have done your duty, depart in peace. I know what has to be done now".

At that moment the keeper came outside again.

"He is past speaking," he said "but he gave me to understand by a sign that he has put all his affairs in order. Nicodemus Pania," he added, turning towards the grandson, "can you assure us on your conscience that we may leave here with quiet minds?"

"Except for the holy sacrament of extreme unction, you need not have come at all. What business have you to meddle in my affairs?" answered the grandson truculently.

"We must carry out the law! And don't raise your voice like that, Nicodemus Pania!" retorted the keeper.

"Enough, enough, no shouting" said the priest, pointing to the hut.

"You are always teaching that there is only one duty in life, and that is to do one's own duty" said the keeper sententiously.

Paul sprang to his feet, struck by those words. Everything he heard now seemed meant specially for him, and he thought God was making known His will through the mouths of men. He mounted his horse and said to the old man's grandson: "Stay with your grandfather until he is dead. God is great and we never know what may happen".

The man accompanied him part of the way, and when they were out of earshot of the keeper he said: "Listen, sir. My grandfather did give his money into my charge; it's here, inside my coat. It is not much, but whatever it is, it belongs to me, doesn't it?".

"If your grandfather gave it to you for yourself alone, then it is yours" replied Paul, turning round to see if the others were following.

They were following. Antiochus was leaning on a stick he had fashioned for himself out of the branch of a tree, and the keeper, the glazed peak of his cap and the buttons of his tunic reflecting the last rays of the evening light, had halted at the corner of the path and was giving the military salute in the direction of the hut. He was saluting death, And from his rocky perch the eagle answered the salute with a last flap of his great wings before he too went to sleep.

The shades of night crept rapidly up from the valley and soon enveloped the three wayfarers. When they had crossed the river, however, and had turned into the path that led up towards home, their road was lit up by a distant glare that came from the village itself. It looked as if the whole place were on fire; huge flames were leaping on the summit of the ridge, and the keeper's keen sight distinguished numerous figures moving about in the square in front of the church. It was a Saturday, and nearly all the men would have returned to their homes for the Sunday rest, but this did not explain the reason for the bonfires and the unusual excitement in the village.

"I know what it is!" called Antiochus joyfully. "They are waiting for us to come back, and they are going to celebrate the miracle of Nina Masia!"

"Good heavens! Are you quite mad, Antiochus?" cried the priest, with something akin to terror as he gazed at the hill-side below the village, over which the bonfires were casting their lurid glare.

The keeper made no remark, but in contemptuous silence he rattled the dog's chain and the animal barked loudly. Whereupon hoarse shouts and yells echoed through the valley, and to the priest in his misery it seemed as though some mysterious voice were protesting against the way in which he had imposed on the simplicity of his parishioners.

"What have I done to them?" he asked himself. "I have made fools of them just as I have made a fool of myself. May God save us all!"

Suggestions for heroic action rushed into his mind. When he reached the village he would stop in the midst of his people and confess his sin; he would tear open his breast before them all and show them his wretched heart, consumed with grief, but burning more fiercely with the flame of his anguish than the fires of brushwood upon the ridge.

But here the voice of his conscience spoke: "It is their faith that they are celebrating. They are glorifying God in thee and thou hast no right to thrust thyself and thy wretchedness between them and God".

But from deeper still within him another voice made itself heard: "It is not that. It is because thou art base and vile and art afraid of suffering, of burning in very truth".

And the nearer they came to the village and the men, the more abased did Paul feel. As the leaping flames fought with the shadows on the hill-side so light and darkness seemed to fight in his conscience, and he did not know what to do. He remembered his first arrival in the village years ago, with his mother following him anxiously as she had followed the first steps of his infancy.

"And I have fallen in her sight" he groaned. "She thinks she has raised me up again, but I am wounded to death."

Then suddenly he bethought him, with a sense of relief, that this improvised festival would help him out of his difficulty and avert the danger he feared.

"I will invite some of them to the presbytery to spend the evening, and they are sure to stay late. If I can get through this night I shall be safe."

The black figures of the men leaning over the parapet of the square could now be distinguished, and higher up, behind the church, the flames of the bonfires were waving in the air like long red flags. The bells were not ringing as on that former occasion, but the melancholy sound of a concertina accompanied the general uproar.

All at once from the top of the church tower there shot up a silver star, which instantly broke into a thousand sparks with an explosion that echoed through the valley. A shout of delight went up from the crowd, followed by another brilliant shower of sparks and the noise of shots being fired. They were letting off their guns in sign of rejoicing, as they did on the nights of the great feasts.

"They have gone mad" said the keeper, and he ran off at full speed in advance, the dog barking fiercely as though there were some revolt to be quelled up there.

Antiochus, on the other hand, felt inclined to weep. He looked at the priest sitting straight upright on his horse and thought he resembled some saint carried in procession. Nevertheless, his reflections took a practical turn: "My mother will do good business tonight with all these merry folk!".

And he felt so happy that he unfolded the cope and threw it over his shoulders. Then he wanted to carry the box again, though he would not give up his new stick, and thus he entered the village looking like one of the Three Kings.

The old hunter's granddaughter called to the priest from her door and asked for news of her grandfather.

"All is well" said Paul.

"Then grandfather is better, is he?"

"Your grandfather is dead by this time."

She gave a scream, and that was the only discordant note of the festival.

The boys had already gone down the hill to meet the priest; they swarmed round his horse like a cloud of flies, and all went up together to the church square. The people there were not so numerous as they had looked from a distance, and the presence of the keeper with his dog had infused some sort of order into the proceedings. The men were ranged round the parapet underneath the trees and some were drinking in front of the little wine-shop kept by the mother of Antiochus: the women, their sleeping infants in their arms, were sitting on the church steps, and in the midst of them sat Nina Masia, as quiet now as a drowsy cat.

In the centre of the square stood the keeper with his dog, as stiff as a statue.

On the arrival of the priest they all got up and gathered round him; but the horse, secretly spurred by its rider, started forward towards a street on the opposite side from the church, where was the house of its master. Whereupon the master, who happened to be one of the men drinking in front of the wine-shop, came forward glass in hand and caught the animal by the bridle.

"Heh, nag, what are you thinking of? Here I am!"

The horse stopped immediately, nuzzling towards its master as if it wanted to drink the wine in his glass. The priest made a movement to dismount, but the man held him fast by one leg, while he led horse and rider in front of the wine-shop, where he stretched out his glass to a companion who was holding the bottle.

The whole crowd, men and women, now formed a circle round the priest. In the lighted doorway of the wine-shop, smiling at the scene, stood the tall, gipsy-like figure of Antiochus's mother, her face almost bronze-coloured in the reflection of the bonfires. The babies had wakened up startled and were struggling in their mothers' arms, the gold and coral amulets with which all, even the poorest, was adorned, gleaming as they moved. And in the centre of this restless throng, confused grey figures in the darkness, sat the priest high upon his horse, in very truth like a shepherd in the midst of his flock.

A white-bearded old man placed his hand on Paul's knee and turned towards the people.

"Good folk," he said in a voice shaking with emotion, "this is truly a man of God!"

"Then drink to a good vintage!" cried the owner of the horse offering the glass, which Paul accepted and immediately put to his lips; but his teeth shook against the edge of the glass as though the red wine glowing in the light of the fires were not wine, but blood.

Paul was seated again at his own table in the little dining-room, lighted by an oil lamp. Behind the ridge, which looked a mountain as seen from the presbytery window, the full moon was rising in the pale sky.

He had invited several of the villagers to come in and keep him company, amongst them the old man with the white beard and the owner of the horse, and they were still sitting there drinking and joking, and telling hunting stories. The old man with the white beard, a hunter himself, was criticizing King Nicodemus because, in his opinion, the old recluse did not conduct his hunting according to the law of God.

"I don't want to speak ill of him in his last hour," he was saying; "but to tell the truth, he went out hunting simply as a speculation. Now last winter he must have made thousands of lire by marten skins alone. God allows us to shoot animals, but not to exterminate them! And he used to snare them, too, and that is forbidden, because animals feel pain just as we do, and the hours they lie caught in the snares must be terrible. Once I myself, with these very eyes, I saw a snare where a hare had left her foot. Do you understand what that means? The hare had been caught in the snare and had gnawed the flesh away all round her foot, and had broken her leg off to get free. And what did Nicodemus do with his money, after all? He hid it, and now his grandson will drink it all in a few days."

"Money is made to be spent," said the owner of the horse, a man much given to boasting; "I myself, for instance, I have always spent freely and enjoyed myself, without hurting anyone. Once at our festival, having nothing else to do, I stopped a man who sold silk reels and happened to be passing with a load of his goods; I bought the whole lot, then I set them rolling about on the piazza and ran after them, kicking them here and there and everywhere! In one instant the whole crowd was after me, laughing and yelling, and the boys and young men, and even some of the older men began to imitate me. That was a game that's not forgotten yet! Every time the old priest saw me he used to shout from ever so far: «Hallo, Pasquale Masia, haven't you any reels to set rolling today?»".

All the guests laughed at the tale, only Paul seemed absent-minded and looked pale and tired. The old man with the white beard, who was observing him with reverent affection, winked at his companions to suggest an immediate departure. It was time to leave the servant of God to his holy solitude and well-merited repose.

The guests rose from their seats all together and took respectful leave of their host; and Paul found himself alone, between the flickering flame of the oil lamp and the calm splendour of the moon that shone in through the high window, while the sound of the heavy iron-shod shoes of his departing guests echoed down the deserted street.

It was yet early to go to bed, and although he was utterly worn out and his shoulders ached with fatigue, as though he had been bearing a heavy yoke all the day, he had no thought of going up to his own room. His mother was still in the kitchen: he could not see her from where he sat, but he knew that she was watching as on *the previous night*.

The previous night! He felt as if he had been suddenly awakened out of a long sleep, and the distress of his return home from the house of Agnes, and his thoughts in the night, the letter, the Mass, the journey up the mountain, the villagers' demonstration, had all been only a dream. His real life was beginning again now: he had but to take a step, a dozen steps, to open the door... and go back to her... His real life was beginning again.

"But perhaps she is not expecting me any longer. Perhaps she will never expect me again!"

Then he felt his knees trembling and terror took hold of him again, not at the thought of going back to her, but at the thought that she might have accepted her fate and be already beginning to forget him.

Then he realized that in the depths of his heart the hardest thing to bear since he came down from the mountain had been this and not knowing anything about her, her silence, her vanishing out of his life.

This was the veritable death, that she should cease to love him.

He buried his face in his hands and tried to bring her image before his mind's eye, then he began to reproach her for those things for which she might justly have reproached him.

"Agnes, you cannot forget your promises! How can you forget them? You held my wrists in your two strong hands and said to me: «We are bound to each other forever, in life and in death». Is it possible that you can forget? You said, you know..."

His fingers gripped at his collar, for he was suffocating with his distress.

"The devil has caught me in his snare" he thought, and remembered the hare which had gnawed off her own foot.

He drew a deep breath, rose from his chair, and took up the lamp. He determined to conquer his will, to gnaw his own flesh also if thereby he could only free himself. Now he decided to go up to his room, but as he moved towards the hall he saw his mother sitting in her accustomed place in the silent kitchen, and beside her was Antiochus fast asleep. He went to the door.

"Why is that boy still here?" he asked.

His mother looked at him hesitatingly: she would have preferred not to answer, but to have hidden Antiochus behind her wide skirts in order that Paul should not wait up any longer, but go to his room and to bed. Her faith in him was now completely restored, but she too thought of the devil and his snares. At this moment, however, Antiochus woke up and remembered very well why he was still waiting there, in spite of the fact that the woman had several times asked him to go.

"I was waiting here because my mother is expecting a visit from you" he explained.

"But is this a time of night to go paying visits?" protested the priest's mother. "Come now, be off with you, and tell her that Paul is tired and will go and see her tomorrow."

She spoke to the boy, but she was looking at her son: she saw his glassy eyes fixed upon the lamp, but his eyelids quivered like the wings of a moth in a candle.

Antiochus got up with an expression of deep disappointment.

"But my mother is expecting him; she thinks it's something important."

"If it was anything important he would go and tell her at once. Come, be off with you!"

She spoke sharply, and as Paul looked at her his eyes lit up again with quick resentment: he saw that his mother was afraid lest he should go out again, and the knowledge filled him with unreasoning anger. He banged the lamp down on the table again and called to Antiochus: "We will go and see your mother".

In the hall, however, he turned and added: "I shall be back directly, mother; don't fasten the door".

She had not moved from where she sat, but when the two had left the house she went to peep through the half-open door and saw them cross the moonlit square and enter the wine-shop, which was still lighted up. Then she went back to the kitchen and began her vigil as on the previous night.

She marvelled at herself to find that she was no longer afraid of the old priest reappearing; it had all been a dream. At the bottom of her heart, however, she did not feel at all certain that the ghost would not come back and demand his mended socks.

"I have mended them all right" she said aloud, thinking of those she had mended for her son. And she felt that even if the ghost did come back she would be able to hold her own with him and keep on friendly terms.

Complete silence reigned all round. Outside the window the trees shone silver in the bright moonlight, the sky was like a milky sea, and the perfume of the aromatic shrubs penetrated even into the house. And the mother herself was tranquil now, though she hardly knew why, seeing that Paul might yet fall again into sin; but she no longer felt the same terror of it. She saw again in her mind's eye the lashes trembling on his cheeks, like those of a child about to cry, and her mother's heart melted with tenderness and pity.

"And why, oh Lord, why, why?"

She dared not complete her question, but it remained at the bottom of her heart like a stone at the bottom of a well. Why, oh Lord, was Paul forbidden to love a woman? Love was lawful for all, even for servants and herdsmen, even for the blind and for convicts in prison; so why should Paul, her child, be the only one to whom love was forbidden?

Then again the consciousness of reality forced itself on her. She remembered the words of Antiochus, and was ashamed of being less wise than a boy.

«They themselves, the youngest amongst the priests, asked permission to live chaste and free, apart from women.»

Moreover, her Paul was a strong man, in no wise inferior to his ancient predecessors. He would never give way to tears; his eyelids would close over eyes dry as those of the dead, for he was a strong man.

"I am growing childish!" she sobbed.

She felt as if she had grown twenty years older in that one long day of wearing emotions: each hour that passed had added to the burden she bore, each minute had struck a blow upon her soul as the hammer of the stone-breaker struck upon the heaps of broken rock there behind the ridge. So many things now seemed clear to her, different from on the previous day. The figure of Agnes came before her, with the proud look that concealed all she really felt.

"She is strong too," thought the mother "she will hide everything."

Then slowly she rose from her chair and began to cover the fire with ashes, banking it up carefully so that no sparks could fly out and set fire to anything near: then she shut the house door, for she knew Paul always carried a key with him. She stamped about loudly, as though he could hear her across the square, and believe her firm footsteps to be an outward sign of her inward assurance.

She felt, however, that this assurance was not so very firm after all. But then what is really firm in this life? Neither the base of the mountains nor the foundations of the churches, for an earthquake may overthrow them both. Thus she felt sure of Paul for the future, and sure of herself, but always with an underlying dread of the unknown which might chance to supervene. And when she reached her bedroom she dropped wearily into a chair, wondering whether it would not have been better after all to leave the front door open.

Then she got up and began to untie her apron string; but it had twisted into a knot over which she lost patience at last, and went to fetch a pair of scissors from her work-basket. She found the kitten curled up asleep inside the basket, and the scissors and reels were all warm from contact with its tiny body; and somehow the touch of the living thing made her repent of her impatience, and she went back to the lamp, and drawing the knot in front of her she succeeded at last in untying it. With a sigh of relief she slowly undressed, carefully folding her garments one by one on the chair, first, however, taking the keys out of her apron pocket and laying them in a row on the table like a respectable family all asleep. Thus her masters had taught her in her youth to cultivate order and tidiness, and she still obeyed the old instructions.

She sat down again, half undressed, her short chemise displaying thin brown legs that might have been made of wood, and she yawned with weariness and resignation. No, she would not go downstairs again; her son should come home and find the door closed, and see from that fact that his mother had full confidence in him. That was the right way to manage him, show that you trusted him absolutely. Nevertheless, she was on the alert, and listened for the least sound; not in the same way as on the previous night, but still she listened. She drew off her shoes and placed them side by side, like two sisters who must keep each other company even during the night, and went on murmuring her prayers and yawning, yawning with weariness and resignation, and with sheer nervousness, too.

Whatever could Paul have to say to Antiochus's mother? The woman had by no means a good reputation, she lent money on usury and was commonly supposed to be a procuress too. No, Paul's mother could not understand it. Then she blew out the candle, snuffed the smoking wick with her fingers and got into bed, but could not bring herself to lie down.

Presently she thought she heard a step in her room. Was it the ghost come back? She was filled with a horrible fear lest he should come up to the bed and take hold of her; for a moment her blood froze in her veins, then surged to her heart as a people in tumult rushes through the streets of its city to the principal square. Then she recovered herself and was ashamed of her fear, only caused, she was sure, by the wicked doubts she had entertained of her Paul.

No, those doubts were all ended: never again would she inquire into the very smallest of his actions; it was her place to keep quietly in the background, as she was now, in her little room fit only for a servant. She lay down and drew the bedclothes over her, covering her ears, too, so that she might not hear whether Paul came home or not; but in her inner consciousness she *felt* all the same, she felt that he was not coming home, that he had been carried off by someone against his will, as one drawn reluctantly into a dance.

Nevertheless she felt quite sure of him; sooner or later he would manage to escape and come home. Anyhow, she was resting quietly under the bedclothes, though not yet asleep, and she had a confused impression that she was still trying to undo the knot in her apron string. Then the faint buzzing in her ears beneath the coverlet turned gradually into the murmuring of the crowd in the square beneath her window, and farther off still the murmuring of a people who lamented, and yet whilst lamenting laughed and danced and sang. Her Paul was there in the midst of them, and above them all in some high, far place, a lute was being softly played. Perhaps it was God Himself playing to the dance of men.

All day long Antiochus's mother had been speculating as to what could be the object of the priest's visit, for which her boy had prepared her, but she took good care not to betray by her manner that she was expecting him. Perhaps he intended making a few remarks on the subject of usury, and certain other trades which she practised; or because she was in the habit of lending out – for purely medical purposes, but always for a small fee – certain very ancient relics which she had inherited from her husband's family.

Or perhaps he wanted to borrow money, either for himself or someone else. Whatever it might prove to be, as soon as the last customer had departed she went to the door and stood there with her hands in her pockets, heavy with copper coins, looking out to see whether Antiochus at least were not in sight.

Then immediately she pretended to be busy shutting the door, and in fact she did shut the lower half, bending down to fasten the bolt. She was active in her movements, although tall and stout; but, contrary to the other women of the place, she had a small head, which only looked large because of the great mass of black plaits that encircled it.

As the priest approached she drew herself up and bade him good evening with much dignity, though her black eyes looked straight into his with an ardent, languorous gaze. Then she invited him to take a seat in the room behind the wine-shop, and Antiochus's wistful eyes begged her to press the invitation. But the priest said good-humouredly: "No, let us stay here" and he sat down at one of the long, wine-stained tables that furnished the little tavern, whilst Antiochus, resigned to the inevitable, stood beside him, casting anxious glances round, however, to see if everything was in order and fearful lest any belated customer should come in to disturb the conference.

Nobody came and everything was in order. The big petroleum lamp threw an immense shadow of his mother on the wall behind the little bar, covered with shelves filled with bottles of red, yellow and green liqueurs, the light falling crudely on the small black casks ranged along the opposite side of the shop. There was no other furniture except the long table at which sat the priest, and another smaller one, and over the door hung a bunch of broom which served the double purpose of informing passers-by that this was the door of a wine-shop and of attracting flies away from the glasses.

Antiochus had been waiting for this moment during the whole of the day, with the feeling that some mystery would then be revealed. He was afraid of some intruder coming in, or that his mother would not behave as she should. He would have liked her to be more humble, more docile in the presence of the priest; but instead of that she had taken her seat again behind the bar, and sat there as composedly as a queen on her throne. She did not even appear to realize that the man seated at the tavern table like an ordinary customer was a saint who worked miracles, and she was not even grateful for the large quantity of wine which he had been the indirect means of her selling that day!

At last, however, Paul opened the conversation.

"I should have liked to see your husband as well," he began, resting his elbows on the table and placing his finger-tips together, "but Antiochus tells me that he will not be back until Sunday week."

The woman merely nodded in assent.

"Yes, on Sunday week, but I can go and fetch him, if you like" broke in Antiochus, with an eagerness of which neither of the others took the least notice.

"It is about the boy" continued Paul. "The time has come when you must really consider in earnest what you are going to do with him. He is growing big now and you must either teach him a trade or, if you want to make a priest of him, you must think very seriously of the responsibility you are undertaking."

Antiochus opened his lips, but as his mother began to speak he listened to her silently, though with a shade of disapproval on his anxious young face.

The woman seized the occasion, as she always did, to sound the praises of her husband, also to excuse herself for having married a man much older than herself: "My Martin, as your Reverence knows, is the most conscientious man in the world; he is a good husband and a good father and a better workman than anyone else. Who is there in the whole village who works as hard as he does? Tell me that, your Reverence, you who know what sort of a character the village has got through the idleness of its inhabitants! I say, then, that if Antiochus wants to choose a trade, he has only to follow his father's; that is the best trade for him. The boy is free to do as he likes, and even if he wants to do nothing (I don't say it for vanity), he will be able to live without turning thief, thank

God! But if he wants a trade different from his father's, then he must choose for himself. If he wants to be a charcoal-burner, let him be a charcoal-burner; if he wants to be a carpenter, let him be a carpenter; if he wants to be a labourer, let him be a labourer".

"I want to be a priest!" said the boy with quivering lips and eager eyes.

"Very well then, be a priest" replied his mother.

And thus his fate was decided.

Paul let his hands fall upon the table and gazed slowly round him. Quite suddenly he felt it was ridiculous that he should thus interest himself in other people's business. How could he possibly solve the problem of the future for Antiochus when he could not succeed in solving it for himself? The boy stood before him in ardent expectation, like a piece of red-hot iron awaiting the stroke of the hammer to mould it into shape, and every word had the power to either make or mar him. Paul's gaze rested on him with something akin to envy, and in the depths of his conscience he applauded the mother's action in leaving her son free to follow his own instincts.

"Instinct never leads us wrong" he said aloud, following his own train of thought. "But now, Antiochus, tell me in your mother's presence the reason why you wish to be a priest. Being a priest is not a trade, you know; it is not like being a charcoal-burner or a carpenter. You think now that it is a very easy, comfortable kind of life, but later on you will find that it is very difficult. The joys and pleasures allowed to all other men are forbidden to us, and if we truly desire to serve the Lord our life is one continuous sacrifice."

"I know that" replied the boy very simply. "I desire to serve the Lord."

He looked at his mother then, because he was a little ashamed of betraying all his enthusiasm before her, but she sat behind the bar as calmly and coldly as when she was merely serving customers. So Antiochus went on: "Both my father and mother are willing for me to become a priest; why should they object? I am very careless sometimes, but that is because I am still only a boy, and in future I mean to be much more serious and attentive".

"That is not the question, Antiochus; you are too serious and attentive already!" said Paul. "At your age you should be heedless and merry. Learn and prepare yourself for life, certainly, but be a boy too."

"And am I not a boy?" protested Antiochus; "I do play, only you don't happen to see me just when I am playing! Besides, why should I play if I don't feel inclined? I have lots of amusements: I enjoy ringing the church bells and I feel as if I was a bird up in the tower. And haven't I had an amusing time today? I enjoyed carrying the box and climbing up ever so high amongst the rocks, and I got there before you, although you were riding! I enjoyed coming home again... and today I enjoyed... I was happy," and the boy's eyes sought the ground as he added "when you drove the devils out of the body of Nina Masia."

"You believed in that?" asked the priest in a low voice, and immediately he saw the boy's eyes look upward, so glorious with the light of faith and wonder that instinctively he lowered his own to hide the dark shadow that rested on his soul.

"Only, when we are children we think in one way and everything looks great and beautiful to us," continued Paul, much disturbed, "but when we are grown up things look different. One must reflect very carefully before undertaking anything important so that one may not come to repent afterwards."

"I shall not repent, I'm sure" said the boy with decision. "Have you repented? No, and neither shall I repent."

Paul lifted up his eyes: again he felt that he held in his hands the soul of this child, to mould it like wax, and that a few careless touches might deform it forever. And again he feared and was silent.

All this time the woman behind the bar had listened quietly, but now the priest's words began to cause her a certain uneasiness. She opened a drawer in front of her, wherein she kept her money, and the cornelian rings and the brooches and mother-of-pearl ornaments pledged by the village women in return for small loans; and evil thoughts flashed through the darkest recesses of her mind, like those forlorn trinkets at the bottom of her drawer.

"The priest is afraid that Antiochus will turn him out of his parish some time or other," she was thinking "or else he is in need of money and is working off his bad temper first. Now he'll be asking for a loan."

She closed the drawer softly and resumed her tranquil demeanour. She always sat there in silence and never took part in the discussions between her customers, even though invited to give her opinion, especially if they were playing cards. Thus she left her little Antiochus to face his adversary by himself.

"How is it possible not to believe?" said the boy, between awe and excitement. "Nina Masia was possessed, wasn't she? Why, I myself felt the devil inside her shaking her like a wolf in a cage. And it was nothing but the words of the Gospel spoken by you that set her free!"

"That is true, the Word of God can achieve all things" admitted the priest. Then suddenly he rose from his seat.

Was he going? Antiochus gazed at him in consternation.

"Are you going?" he murmured.

Was this the famous visit? He ran to the bar and made a desperate sign to his mother, who turned round and took down a bottle from the shelves. She was disappointed too, for she had hoped for a chance of lending money to the parish priest, even at a very low interest, thereby in some way legitimizing her usury in the sight of God. But instead of that, he had simply come to inform Antiochus that being a priest was not the same thing as being a carpenter! However, she must do him honour, in any case.

"But your Reverence is not going away like that! Accept something to drink, at least; this wine is very old."

Antiochus was already holding the tray with a glass goblet upon it.

"Then only a little" said Paul.

Leaning across the bar, the woman poured out the wine, careful not to spill a drop. Paul raised his glass, within which the ruby liquid exhaled a perfume like a dusky rose, and after first making Antiochus taste it, he put it to his own lips.

"Then let us drink to the future parish priest of Aar!" he said.

Antiochus was obliged to lean against the bar, for his knees gave way under him; that was the happiest moment of his life. The woman had turned round to replace the precious bottle on the shelf, and, absorbed in his joy, the lad did not notice that the priest had gone deathly pale and was staring out of the doorway as though he beheld a ghost.

A dark figure was running silently across the square, came to the wine-shop door, looked round the interior with wide-open black eyes, and then entered, panting.

It was one of Agnes's servants.

The priest instinctively withdrew to the far end of the tavern, trying to hide himself, then came forward again on a sudden impulse. He felt as if he were revolving round and round like a top, then pulled himself together and remembered that he was not alone and must be careful not to excite remark. So he stood still. But he had no desire to hear what the servant was telling the woman, listening eagerly behind the bar, his only desire was flight and safety; his heart had stopped beating, and all the blood in his body had rushed to his head and was roaring in his ears. Nevertheless the servant's words penetrated to the utmost depths of his soul.

"She fell down," said the girl breathlessly "and the blood poured from her nose in a stream, such a stream that we thought she had broken something inside her head! And she's bleeding still! Give me the keys of St. Mary of Egypt, for that is the only thing that can stop it."

Antiochus, who stood listening with the tray and glass still in his hands, ran to fetch the keys of an old church, now demolished, which keys when actually laid on the shoulders of anyone suffering from haemorrhage of the nose did to some extent arrest the flow of blood.

"All this is just pretence," thought Paul "there is no truth whatever in the tale. She sent her servant to spy on me and endeavour to lure me to her house, and they are probably in league with this worthless woman here."

And yet deep, deep within him the agitation grew till all his being was in a tumult. Ah, no, the servant was not lying; Agnes was too proud to confide in anyone, and least of all in her servants. Agnes was really ill, and with his inward eye he saw her sweet face all stained with blood. And it was he himself who had struck her the blow. "We thought she had broken something inside her head."

He saw the shifty eyes of the woman behind the bar glance swiftly in his direction, with obvious surprise at his apparent indifference.

"But how did it happen?" he then asked the servant, but coolly and calmly, as though seeking to conceal his anxiety even from himself.

The girl turned and confronted him, her dark, hard, pointed face thrust out towards him like a rock against which he feared to strike.

"I was not at home when she fell. It happened this morning whilst I was at the fountain, and when I got back I found her very ill. She had fallen over the doorstep and blood was flowing from her nose, but I think she was more frightened than hurt. Then the blood stopped, but she was very pale all day and refused to eat. Then this evening her nose began to bleed again, and not only that, but she had a sort of convulsion, and when I left her just now she was lying cold and stiff, with blood still flowing. I am very nervous," added the girl, taking the keys which Antiochus handed to her and wrapping them in her apron, "and we are only women in the house."

She moved towards the door, but kept her black eyes on Paul as though seeking to draw him after her by the sheer power of her gaze, and the woman seated behind the bar said in her cold voice: "Why does not your Reverence go and see her?".

He wrung his hands unconsciously and stammered: "I hardly know... it is too late...".

"Yes, come, come!" urged the servant. "My little mistress will be very glad, and it will give her courage to see you."

"It is the devil speaking by your mouth" thought Paul, but unconsciously he followed the girl. He had gripped Antiochus by the shoulder and was drawing him along as a support, and the boy went with him like a plank of safety upon the waves. So they

crossed the square and went as far as the presbytery, the servant
running on ahead, but turning every few steps to look back at
them, the whites of her eyes gleaming in the moonlight. Seen thus
at night, the black figure with the dark and mask-like face had
truly something diabolical about it, and Paul followed it with a
vague sense of fear, leaning on Antiochus's shoulder as he walked
and feeling like Tobit in his blindness.

On passing the presbytery door the boy tried to open it, and
then Paul perceived that his mother had locked it. He stopped
short and disengaged himself from his companion.

"My mother has locked up because she knew in advance that
I should not keep my word" he thought to himself. Then he said
to the boy: "Antiochus, you must go home at once".

The servant had stopped also, then went on a few steps, then
stopped again and saw the boy returning towards his own home
and the priest inserting his key in his door; then she went back
to him.

"I am not coming," he said, turning almost threateningly to
confront her, and looking her straight in the face as though trying to recognize her true nature through her outward mask; "if
you should absolutely need me, you understand – only if you do
absolutely need me – you can come back and fetch me."

She went away without another word, and he stood there
before his own door, with his hand on the key as though it had
refused to turn in the lock. He could not bring himself to enter, it
was beyond his power; neither could he go forward in that other
path he had begun to tread. He felt as if he were doomed to stand
there for all eternity, before a closed door of which he held the key.

Meanwhile Antiochus had reached home. His mother locked
the door and he went to wash up the glasses and put them away;
and the first glass he washed in the clean water was the one from
which *he* had drunk. The boy dried it very carefully with a white
cloth, which he passed round and round inside with his thumb;
then he held it up to the flame of the lamp and examined it with
one eye, keeping the other screwed up, which had the effect of
making the glass shine like a big diamond. Then he hid it away in

a secret cupboard of his own with as much reverence as if it had been the chalice of the Mass.

Paul had gone home too, and was feeling his way upstairs in the dark: he dimly remembered going up some stairs in the dark like this when he was a boy, but he could not remember where it had been. Now, as then, he had the feeling that there was some danger near him which he could only escape by strict attention to what he was doing. He reached the landing, he stood before his own door, he was safe. But he hesitated an instant before opening it, then crossed over and tapped lightly with the knuckle of his forefinger at his mother's door and entered without waiting for a reply.

"It is I," he said brusquely "don't light the candle, I have something to tell you."

He heard her turning round in her bed, the straw mattress creaking under her: but he could not see her, he did not want to see her; their two souls must speak together in the darkness as though they had already passed to the world beyond.

"Is it you, Paul? I was dreaming," she said in a sleepy yet frightened voice "I thought I heard dancing, someone playing on the flute."

"Mother, listen" he said, paying no attention to her words. "That woman, Agnes, is ill. She has been ill since this morning. She had a fall; it seems she hurt her head and is bleeding from her nose."

"You don't mean it, Paul? Is she in danger?"

In the darkness her voice sounded alarmed, yet at the same time incredulous. He went on, repeating the breathless words of the servant: "It happened this morning, after she got the letter. All day long she was pale and refused to eat, and this evening she grew worse and fell into convulsions".

He knew that he was exaggerating, and stopped: his mother did not speak. For a moment in the silence and the night there was a deathlike tension, as though two enemies were seeking each other in the darkness and seeking in vain. Then the straw mattress creaked again; his mother must have raised herself to a sitting position in the high bed, because her clear voice now seemed to come from above.

"Paul, who told you all this? Perhaps it is not true."

Again he felt that it was his conscience speaking to him through her, but he answered at once:

"It may be true. But that is not the question, mother. It is that I fear she may commit some folly. She is alone in the hands of servants, and I must see her."

"Paul!"

"I must," he repeated, raising his voice almost to a shout; but it was himself he was trying to convince, not his mother.

"Paul, you promised!"

"I know I promised, and for that very reason I have come to tell you before I go. I tell you that it is necessary that I should go to her; my conscience bids me go."

"Tell me one thing, Paul: are you sure you saw the servant? Temptation plays evil tricks on us and the devil has many disguises."

He did not quite understand her.

"You think I am telling a lie? I saw the servant."

"Listen to me, last night I saw the old priest and I thought I heard his footsteps again just now. Last night," she went on in a low voice "he sat beside me before the fire. I actually saw him, I tell you: he had not shaved, and the few teeth he had left were black from too much smoking. And he had holes in his stockings. And he said, «I am alive and I am here, and very soon I shall turn you and your son out of the presbytery». And he said I ought to have taught you your father's trade if I did not wish you to fall into sin. He so upset my mind, Paul, that I don't know whether I have acted rightly or wrongly! But I am absolutely sure that it was the devil sitting beside me last night, the spirit of evil. The servant you saw might have been temptation in another shape."

He smiled in the darkness. Nevertheless, when he thought of the fantastic figure of the servant running across the meadow, he felt a vague sense of terror in spite of himself.

"If you go there," continued his mother's voice "are you certain you will not fall again? Even if you really saw the servant and if that woman is really ill, are you sure not to fall?"

She broke off suddenly; she seemed to see his pale face through the darkness, and she was filled with pity for him. Why should she forbid him to go to the woman? Supposing Agnes really died of grief? Supposing Paul died of grief? And she was as wracked with uncertainty as he had been in the case of Antiochus.

"Lord" she sighed; then she remembered that she had already placed herself in the hands of God, Who alone can solve all our difficulties. She felt a sort of relief, as if she had really settled the problem. And had she not settled it by entrusting it in the hands of God?

She lay back on her pillow and her voice came again nearer to her son.

"If your conscience bids you go, why did you not go at once instead of coming in here?"

"Because I promised. And you threatened to leave me if I went back to that house. I swore..." he said with infinite sadness. And he longed to cry out «Mother, force me to keep my oath!» but the words would not come.

And then she spoke again: "Then go: do whatever your conscience bids you".

"Do not be anxious" he said, coming close up to the bed; and he stood there motionless for a few minutes and both were silent. He had a confused impression that he was standing before an altar with his mother lying upon it like some mysterious idol, and he remembered how, when he was a boy in the Seminary, he was always obliged to go and kiss her hand after he had been to confession. And something of the same repugnance and the same exaltation moved him now. He felt that if he had been alone, without her, he would have gone back to Agnes long since, worn out by that endless day of flight and strife; but his mother held him in check, and he did not know whether he was grateful to her or not.

"Do not be anxious!" Yet all the time he longed and feared that she would say more to him, or that she would light the lamp and, looking into his eyes, read all his thoughts and forbid him to go. But she said nothing. Then the mattress creaked again as she stretched herself in the bed.

And he went out.

He reflected that after all he was not a scoundrel: he was not going with any bad motive or moved by passion, but because he honestly thought that there might be some danger he could avert, and the responsibility for this danger rested upon him. He recalled the fantastic figure of the servant running across the moonlit grass, and turning back to look at him with bright eyes as she said: "My little mistress will take courage if only you will come".

And all his efforts to break away from her appeared now base and stupid: his duty was to have gone to her at once and given her courage. And as he crossed the meadow, silvery in the moonlight, he felt relieved, almost happy, he was like a moth attracted by the light. And he mistook the joy he felt at the prospect of seeing Agnes again in a few moments for the satisfaction of doing his duty in going to save her. All the sweet scent of the grass, all the tender radiance of the moon bathed and purified his soul, and the healing dew fell upon it even through his clothes of death-like black.

Agnes, little mistress! In truth, she was little, weak as a child, and she was all alone, without father or mother, living in that labyrinth of stone, her dark house under the ridge. And he had taken advantage of her, had caught her in his hand like a bird from the nest, gripping her till the blood seemed driven from her body.

He hurried on. No, he was not a bad man, but as he reached the bottom of the steps that led up to the door he stumbled, and it was sharply borne in upon him that even the stones of her threshold repulsed him. Then he mounted softly, hesitatingly, raised the knocker and let it fall. They were a long time coming to answer the door, and he felt humiliated standing there, but for nothing in the world would he have knocked a second time. At last the fanlight over the door was lit up and the dark-faced maid let him in, showing him at once into the room he knew so well.

Everything was just as it had been on other nights, when Agnes had admitted him secretly by way of the orchard; the little door stood ajar, and through the narrow opening he could smell the fragrance of the bushes in the night air. The glass eyes in the stuffed heads of stags and deer on the walls shone in the steady glow of the big lamp, as though taking careful note of all that happened in the room. Contrary to custom, the door leading to the inner rooms stood wide open; the servant had gone through there and the board flooring could be heard creaking under her heavy step. After a moment a door banged violently as though blown by a gust of wind, making the whole house shake, and he started involuntarily when immediately afterwards he beheld Agnes emerge from the darkness of the inner rooms, with white face and distorted hair floating in black wisps across it, like the phantom of a drowned woman. Then the little figure came forward into the lamplight and he almost sobbed with relief.

She closed the door behind her and leaned against it with bowed head. She faltered as though about to fall, and Paul ran to her, holding out his hands, but not daring to touch her.

"How are you?" he asked in a low voice, as he had asked at former meetings. But she did not answer, only stood trembling all over her body, her hands pressed against the door behind her for support. "Agnes," he continued after a moment's tense silence "we must be brave."

But as on that day when he had read the Gospel words over the frenzied girl, he knew that his voice rang false, and his eyes sought the ground as Agnes raised hers, bewildered, yes, but full of mingled scorn and joy.

"Then why have you come?"

"I heard that you were ill."

She drew herself up proudly and pushed back the hair from her face.

"I am quite well and I did not send for you."

"I know that, but I came all the same. There was no reason why I should not come. I am glad to find that your maid exaggerated, and that you are all right."

"No," she repeated, interrupting him "I did not send for you and you ought not to have come. But since you are here, since you are here, I want to ask you why you did it... Why? Why?"

Her words were broken by sobs and her hands sought blindly for support, so that Paul was afraid, and repented that he had come. He took her hands and led her to the couch where they had sat together on other evenings, placing her in the corner where the weight of other women of the family had worn a sort of niche, and seated himself beside her, but he let go her hands.

He was afraid of touching her; she was like a statue which he had broken and put together again, and which sat there apparently whole but ready to fall in pieces again at the slightest movement. So he was afraid of touching her, and he thought to himself: "It is better so, I shall be safe" but in his heart he knew that at any moment he might be lost again, and for that reason he was afraid of touching her. Looking closely at her beneath the lamplight, he perceived that she was changed. Her mouth was half-open, her lips discoloured and greyish like faded rose-leaves; the oval of her face seemed to have grown longer and her cheekbones stood out sharply beneath eyes sunk deep in their livid sockets. Grief had aged her by twenty years in a single day, yet there was something childlike still in the expression of her trembling lips, drawn tightly over her teeth to check her weeping, and in the little hands, one of which, lying nerveless on the dark stuff of the couch, invited his own towards it. And he was filled with anger because he dared not take that little hand in his and link up again the broken chain of their two lives. He remembered the words of the man possessed with a devil, «What have I to do with Thee?» and he began to speak again, clasping his hands together to prevent himself taking one of hers. But still he heard his voice ring false, and as on that morning in church when he read the Gospel, and when he carried the sacrament to the old hunter, he knew himself to be lying.

"Agnes, listen to me. Last night we were both on the brink of destruction. God had left us to ourselves and we were slipping over the edge of the abyss. But now God has taken us by the hand again and is guiding us. We must not fall, Agnes, Agnes" and his voice shook with emotion as he spoke her name. "You think I don't suffer? I feel as if I were buried alive and that my torments would last through all eternity. But we must endure for your good, for your salvation. Listen, Agnes, be brave, for the sake of the love which united us, for God's goodwill toward us in putting us through this trial. You will forget me. You will recover; you are young, with all your life still before you. When you think of me it will be like a bad dream, as though you had lost your way in the valley and met some evil creature who had tried to do you harm; but God has saved you, as you deserved to be saved. Everything looks black at present, but it will clear up soon and you will realize that I am only acting for your good in causing you a little momentary pain now, just as we are sometimes obliged to seem cruel to those who are ill..."

He stopped, the words froze in his throat.

Agnes had roused herself and was sitting upright in her corner, gazing at him with eyes as glassy as those in the stags' heads on the walls. They reminded him of the women's eyes in church, fixed on him as he preached. She waited for his words, patient and gentle in every line of her fragile form, yet ready to break down at a touch. Then speechless himself, he heard her low voice as she shook her head slowly.

"No, no, that is not the truth" she said.

"Then what is the truth?" he asked, bending his troubled face towards her.

"Why did you not speak like that last night? And the other nights? Because it was a different kind of truth then. Now somebody has found you out, perhaps your mother herself, and you are afraid of the world. It is not the fear of God which is driving you away from me!"

He wanted to cry out, to strike her; he seized her hand and twisted the slender wrist as he would have liked to twist and stifle the words she spoke. Then he drew himself up stiffly.

"What then? You think it does not matter? Yes, my mother has discovered everything and she talked to me like my conscience itself. And have you no conscience? Do you think it right that we should injure those who depend on us? You wanted us to go away and live together, and that would have been the right thing to do if we had not been able to overcome our love; but since there are beings who would have been cut off from life by our flight and our sin, we had to sacrifice ourselves for them."

But she seemed not to understand, caught only one word, and shook her head as before.

"Conscience? Of course I have a conscience, I am no longer a child! And my conscience tells me that I did wrong in listening to you and letting you come here. What is to be done? It is too late now; why did not God make you see things clearly at first? I did not go to your home, but you came to mine and played with me as if I had been a child's toy. And what must I do now? Tell me that. I cannot forget you, I cannot change as you change. I shall go away, even if you will not come with me. I want to try and forget you. I must go right away, or else..."

"Or else?"

Agnes did not reply; she leaned back in her corner and shivered. Something ominous, like the dark wing of madness, must have touched her, for her eyes grew dim and she raised her hand with an instinctive movement as though to brush away a shadow from before her face. He bent again towards her, stretching across the couch and his fingers gripping and breaking through the old material as though it were a wall that rose between them and threatened to stifle him.

He could not speak. Yes, she was right; the explanation he had been trying to make her believe was not the truth. It was the truth that was rising like a wall and stifling him, and which he did not know how to break down. And he sat up, battling with a real sense of suffocation. Now it was she who caught his hand and held it as though her fingers had been grappling-hooks.

"Oh God," she whispered, covering her eyes with her free hand, "if there be a God, He should not have let us meet each other if we must part again. And you came tonight because you love me still. You think I don't know that? I do know, I do know, and that is the truth!"

She raised her face to his, her trembling lips, her lashes wet with tears. And his eyes were dazzled as by the glitter of deep waters, a glitter that blinds and beckons, and the face he gazed into was not the face of Agnes, nor the face of any woman on this earth, it was the face of Love itself. And he fell forward into her arms and kissed her upon the mouth.

The world had ceased for Paul. He felt himself sinking slowly, swept down by a whirlpool through luminous depths to some dazzling iridescent place beneath the sea. Then he came to himself again and drew his lips away from hers, and found himself, like a shipwrecked man upon the sand, safe though maimed, and shaking with fear and joy, but more with fear than joy. And the enchantment that he thought had been broken forever, and for this very reason had seemed more beautiful and dear, wove its spell over him afresh and held him again in thrall. And again he heard the whisper of her voice: "I knew you would come back to me…".

He wanted to hear no more, just as he had tried not to hear the servant's tale in the house of Antiochus. He put his hand over Agnes's mouth as she leaned her head upon his shoulder and then gently caressed her hair, on which the lamplight threw golden gleams. She was so small, so helpless in his grasp, and therein lay her terrible power to drag him down to the bottom of the sea, to raise him to the highest heights of heaven, to make of him a thing without will or desire of his own. Whilst he had fled through the valleys and the hills she had remained shut up within her prison-house, waiting in the certainty that he would come back to her, and he came.

"You know, you know…" She tried to tell him more; her soft breath touched his neck like a caress, he placed his hand on her mouth again and with her own she pressed it close. And so they remained in silence for a while; then he pulled himself together and tried to regain the mastery over his fate. He had come back to her, yes, but not the same man she had expected. And his gaze still rested on her gleaming hair, but as on something far away, as on the bright sparkle of the sea from which he had escaped.

"Now you are happy" he whispered. "I am here, I have come back and I am yours for life. But you must be calm, you have given me a great fright. You must not excite yourself, nor wander on any account from the straight path of your life. I shall cause you no more trouble, but you must promise me to be calm and good, as you are now."

He felt her hands tremble and struggle between his own; he divined that she was already beginning to rebel and he held them tightly, as he would have liked to hold her soul imprisoned.

"Dear Agnes, listen! You will never know all I have suffered today, but it was necessary. I stripped off all the outward shell of me, all that was impure, and I scourged myself until I bled. But now here I am, yours, yours, but as God wills that I should be yours, in spirit... You see," he went on, speaking slowly and laboriously, as though dragging his words up painfully from his inmost depths and offering them to her, "it seems to me that we have loved each other for years and years, that we have rejoiced and suffered the one for the other, even unto hatred, even unto death. And all the tempests of the sea and all its implacable life are within us. Agnes, soul of my soul, what wouldst thou have of me greater than that which I can give thee, my soul itself?"

He stopped short. He felt that she did not understand, she could not understand. And he beheld her ever more detached from him, as life from death; but for this very reason he loved her still, yea, more than ever, as one loves life that is dying.

She slowly raised her head from his shoulder and looked him in the face with eyes grown hostile again.

"Now you listen to me," she said "and tell me no more lies. Are we or are we not going away together as we settled last night? We cannot go on living here, in this way. That is certain!... That is certain!" she repeated with rising anger, after a moment of painful silence. "If we are to live together we must go away at once, this very night. I have money, you know, it is my own. And your mother and my brothers and everyone else will excuse us afterwards when they see that we only wanted to live according to the truth. We cannot go on living like this, no, we cannot!"

"Agnes!"

"Answer me quick! Yes or no?"

"I cannot go away with you."

"Ah, then why have you come back?... Leave me! Get away, leave me!"

He did not leave her. He felt her whole body shaking and he was afraid of her; and as she bowed herself over their united hands he expected to feel her teeth fasten in his flesh.

"Go, go!" she insisted. "I did not send for you! Since we must be brave, why did you come back? Why have you kissed me again? Ah, if you think you can play with me like this you are mistaken! If you think you can come here at night and write me humiliating letters in the day you are mistaken again! You came back tonight and you will come back tomorrow night and every night after that, until at last you drive me mad. But I won't have it, I won't have it!"

"We must be pure and brave, you say," she continued, and her face, grown old and tragic, became now pale as death; "but you never said that before tonight. You fill me with horror! Go away, far away, and go at once, so that tomorrow I can wake up without the terror of expecting you and being humiliated like this again."

"Oh God, oh God!" he groaned, bending over her, but she repulsed him sharply.

"Do you think you are speaking to a child?" she burst out now: "I am old, and it is you who have made me grow old in a few hours. The straight path of life! Oh, yes, it would be going straight if we continued this secret intrigue, wouldn't it? I should find myself a husband and you should marry me to him, and then we could go on seeing each other, you and I, and deceiving everyone for the rest of our lives. Oh, you don't know me if that is your idea! Last night you said «Let us go away, we will get married and I will work». Didn't you say that? Didn't you? But tonight you come and talk to me instead about God and sacrifice. So now there is an end of it all: we will part. But you, I say it again, you must leave the village this very night, I never wish to see you again. If tomorrow morning you go once more into our church to say Mass I shall go there too, and from the altar steps I shall say to the people: «This is your saint, who works miracles by day and by night goes to unprotected girls to seduce them!»".

He tried in vain to shut her mouth with his hand, and as she kept on crying aloud, "Go, go!" he seized her head and pressed it to his breast, glancing with alarm at the closed doors. And he remembered his mother's words and her voice, mysterious in the darkness: «The old priest sat beside me and said, I will soon turn both you and your son out of the parish».

"Agnes, Agnes, you are mad!" he groaned, his lips close to her ear, whilst she struggled fiercely to escape from him: "Be calm, listen to me. Nothing is lost; don't you feel how I love you? A thousand times more than before! And I am not going away, I am going to stay near you, to save you, to offer up my soul to you as I shall offer it up to God in the hour of death. How can you know all that I have suffered between last night and now? I fled and I bore you with me: I fled like one who is on fire and who thinks by fleeing to escape the flames which only envelop him the more. Where have I not been today, what have I not done to keep myself from coming back to you? Yet here I am, Agnes, and how could I not be here?... Do you hear me? I shall not betray you, I shall not forget you, I do not wish to forget you! But, Agnes, we must keep ourselves unsoiled, we must keep our love for all eternity, we must unite it with all that is best in life, with renunciation, with death itself, that is to say, with God. Do you understand, Agnes? Yes, tell me that you understand!".

She fought him back, as though she wanted to break in his breast with her head, till at last she freed herself from his embrace and sat rigid and upright, her beautiful hair twisted like ribbons round her stony face. With tight-shut lips and closed eyes, she seemed to have suddenly fallen into a deep sleep, wherein she dreamed of vengeance. And he was more afraid of her silence and immobility than of her frenzied words and excited gestures. He took her hands again in his, but now all four hands were dead to joy and to the clasp of love.

"Agnes, can't you see that I am right? Come, be good; go to bed now and tomorrow a new life will begin for us all. We shall see each other just the same, always supposing you desire it: I will be your friend, your brother, and we shall be a mutual help and support. My life is yours, dispose of me as you wish. I shall be with you till the hour of death, and beyond death, for all eternity."

This tone of prayer irritated her afresh. She twisted her hands slightly within his and opened her lips to speak. Then, as he set her free, she folded her hands in her lap and bowed her head and her face took on an expression of the deepest grief, but now a grief that was desperate and determined.

He continued to gaze steadfastly at her, as one gazes at the dying, and his fear increased. He slid to his knees before her, he laid his head in her lap and kissed her hands; he cared nothing now if he were seen or heard, he knelt there at the feet of the woman and her sorrow as at the feet of the Mother of Sorrows herself. Never before had he felt so pure of evil thought, so dead to this earthly life; and yet he was afraid.

Agnes sat motionless, with icy hands, insensible to those kisses of death. Then he got up and began to speak lies again.

"Thank you, Agnes. That is right and I am very pleased. The trial has been won and you can rest in peace. I am going now, and tomorrow," he added in a whisper, bending nervously towards her, "tomorrow morning you will come to Mass and together we will offer our sacrifice to God."

She opened her eyes and looked at him, then closed them again. She was as one wounded to death, whose eyes had opened wide with a last menace and appeal before they closed forever.

"You will go away tonight, quite away, so that I shall never see you again" she said, pronouncing each word distinctly and decisively, and he realized that for the moment at least it was useless to oppose that blind force.

"I cannot go like that," he murmured: "I must say Mass tomorrow morning and you will come and hear it, and afterwards I will go away, if necessary".

"Then I shall come tomorrow morning and denounce you before all the congregation."

"If you do that it will be a sign that it is God's will. But you won't do it, Agnes! You may hate me, but I leave you in peace. Good-bye."

Even yet he did not go. He stood quite still, looking down at her, at her soft and gleaming hair, the sweet hair he loved and through which so often his hands had strayed, and it awoke in him an infinite pity, for it seemed like the black bandage round a wounded head.

For the last time he called her by her name: "Agnes! Is it possible that we can part like this?... Come," he added after a moment "give me your hand, get up and open the door for me".

She got up obediently, but she did not give him her hand; she went direct to the door through which she had entered the room, and there she stood still, waiting.

"What can I do?" he asked himself. And he knew very well that there was only one thing he could do to appease her: to fall at her feet again, to sin and be lost with her forever.

And that he would not do, never more. He remained firm, there where he stood, and lowered his eyes that he might not meet her look, and when he raised them again she was no longer there; she had disappeared, swallowed up in the darkness of her silent house.

The glass eyes of the stags' and deer's heads upon the walls looked down at him with mingled sadness and derision. And in that moment of suspense, alone in the big melancholy room, he realized the whole immensity of his wretchedness and his humiliation. He felt himself a thief, and worse than a thief, a guest who takes advantage of the solitude of the house that shelters him to rob it basely. He averted his eyes, for he could not meet even the glassy stare of the heads upon the wall: but he did not waver in his purpose for one moment, and even if the death-cry of the woman had suddenly filled the house with horror, he would not have repented having rejected her.

He waited a few minutes longer, but nobody appeared. He had a confused idea that he was standing in the middle of a dead world of all his dreams and his mistakes, waiting till someone came and helped him to get away. But nobody came. So at last he pushed open the door that led into the orchard, traversed the path that ran beside the wall and went out by the little gate he knew so well.

Once more Paul found himself ascending his own staircase; but now the danger was past, or at least the fear of danger.

Nevertheless he halted before his mother's door, deeming that it would be advisable to tell her the result of his interview with Agnes and of her threat to denounce him. But he heard the sound of regular breathing and passed on; his mother had quietly fallen asleep, for henceforth she was sure of him and felt that he was safe.

Safe! He looked round his room as though he had just returned from a long and disastrous journey. Everything was peaceful and tidy, and he moved about on tiptoe as he began to undress, for the sake of not disturbing that orderliness and silence. His clothes hanging from their hooks, blacker than their shadows on the wall, his hat above them, stuck forward on a wooden peg, the sleeves of his cassock falling limply as though tired out, all had the vague appearance of some dark and empty phantom, some fleshless and bloodless vampire that inspired a nameless dread. It was like the shadow of that sin from which he had cut himself free, but which was waiting to follow him again tomorrow on his way through the world.

An instant more, and he perceived with terror that the nightmare obsessed him still. He was not safe yet, there was another night to be got through, as the voyager crosses a last stretch of turbulent sea. He was very weary and his heavy eyelids drooped with fatigue, but an intolerable anxiety prevented him from throwing himself on his bed, or even sitting down on a chair or resting in any way whatever; he wandered here and there, doing small, unusual, useless things, softly opening drawer after drawer and inspecting what there was inside.

As he passed before the mirror he looked at his own reflection and beheld himself grey of face, with purple lips and hollow eyes. "Look at yourself, Paul," he said to his image, and he stepped back a little so that the lamplight might fall better on the glass. The figure in the mirror stepped back also, as though seeking to escape him, and as he stared into its eyes and noted the dilated pupils he had a strange impression that the real Paul was the one in the glass, a Paul who never lied and who betrayed by the pallor of his face all his awful fear of the morrow.

"Why do I pretend even to myself a security which I do not feel?" was his silent question. "I must go away this very night as she bade me."

And somewhat calmer for the resolve he threw himself on his bed. And thus, with closed eyes and face pressed into the pillow, he believed he could search more deeply into his conscience.

"Yes, I must leave tonight. Christ Himself commands us to avoid creating scandals. I had better wake my mother and tell her, and perhaps we can leave together; she can take me away with her again as she did when I was a child and I can begin a new life in another place."

But he felt that all this was mere exaltation and that he had not the courage to do as he proposed. And why should he? He really felt quite sure that Agnes would not carry out her threat, so why should he go away? He was not even confronted with the danger of going back to her and falling into sin again, for he had now been tried and had overcome temptation.

But the exaltation took hold of him again.

"Nevertheless, Paul, you will have to go. Awaken your mother and depart together. Don't you know who it is speaking to you? It is I, Agnes. You really believe that I shall not carry out my threat? Perhaps I shall not, but I advise you to go, all the same. You think you have got rid of me? And yet I am within you, I am the evil genius of your life. If you remain here I shall never leave you alone for one single instant; I shall be the shadow beneath your feet, the barrier between you and your mother, between you and your own self. Go."

Then he tried to pacify her, in order to pacify his own conscience.

"Yes, I am going, I tell you! I am going... We will go together, you within me, more alive than I myself. Be content, torment me no more! We are together, journeying together, borne on the wings of time towards eternity. Divided and distant we were when our eyes first met and our lips kissed; divided were we then and enemies; only now begins our real union, in thy hatred, in my patience, in my renunciation."

Then weariness slowly overcame him. He heard a subdued, continuous moaning outside his window, like a dove seeking her mate: and that mournful cry was like the lament of the night itself, a night pale with moonlight, a soft, veiled light, with the sky all flecked with little white clouds like feathers. Then he became aware that it was he himself who was moaning; but sleep was already stealing over him, calming his senses, and fear and sorrow and remembrance faded away. He dreamed he was really on a journey, riding up the mountain paths towards the plateau. Everything was peaceful and clear; between the big yellow elder trees he could see stretches of grass, of a soft green that gave rest to the eyes, and motionless upon the rocks the eagles blinked at the sun.

Suddenly the keeper stood before him, saluted, and placed an open book on his saddlebow. And he began to read St. Paul's Epistle to the Corinthians, taking it up at the precise point where he had left off the previous night: "The Lord knows the thoughts of the wise and that they are vain".

On Sundays Mass was later than on other days, but Paul always went early to the church to hear the confessions of those women who wished to attend Communion later. So his mother called him at the usual time.

He had slept for some hours, a heavy dreamless sleep, and when he woke his memory was a complete blank, he only had a supreme desire to go to sleep again immediately. But the knocks on his door persisted, and then he remembered. Instantly he was on his feet, numb with dread.

"Agnes will come to church and denounce me before all the people" was his one thought.

He did not know why, but somehow whilst he slept the certainty that she would carry out her threat had taken firm root in his consciousness.

He dropped down in his chair with trembling knees and a sense of complete helplessness. His mind was clouded and confused: he wondered vaguely if it would not be possible even now to avert the scandal. He could feign illness and not say Mass at all, and thus gain time in which he might endeavour to pacify Agnes. But the very idea of beginning the whole thing over again, of suffering a second time all his misery of the previous day, only increased his mental torment.

He got up, and his head seemed to hit the sky through the glass of his window, and he stamped his feet on the floor to dispel the numbness that was paralysing his very blood. Then he dressed, drawing his leather belt tightly round his waist and folding his mantle round him as he had seen the hunters buckle on their cartridge-belts and wrap themselves up in their cloaks before starting out for the mountains. When at last he flung open his window and leaned out he felt that only then were his eyes awaking to the light of day after the nightmare of the dark hours, only then had he escaped from the prison of his own self to make his peace with external things. But it was a forced peace, full of secret rancour, and it sufficed for him to draw in his head from the cool fresh air outside to the warm and perfumed atmosphere of his room for him to fall back into himself, a prey again to his gnawing dread.

So he fled downstairs, wondering what he had better tell his mother.

He heard her somewhat harsh voice driving off the chickens who were trying to invade the dining-room, and the fluttering of their wings as they scattered before her, and he smelt the fragrance of hot coffee and the clean sweet scents from the garden. In the lane under the ridge there was a tinkle of bells as the goats were driven to their pasture, little bells that sounded like childish echoes of the cheerful if monotonous chime wherewith Antiochus, up in the church tower, summoned the people to wake from sleep and come to hear Mass.

Everything around was sweet and peaceful, bathed in the rosy light of early morning. And Paul remembered his dream.

There was nothing to hinder him from going out, from going to church and taking up his ordinary life again. Yet all his fear returned upon him; he was afraid alike of going forward or of turning back. As he stood on the step of the open door he felt as if he were on the summit of some precipitous mountain, it was impossible to get any higher and below him yawned the abyss. So he stood there for unspeakable moments, during which his heart beat furiously and he had the physical sensation of falling, of struggling at the bottom of a gulf, in a swirl of foaming waters, a wheel that turned helplessly, vainly beating the stream that swept on its relentless course.

It was his own heart that turned and turned helplessly in the whirlpool of life. He closed the door and went back into the house, and sat down on the stairs as his mother had done the previous night. He gave up trying to solve the problem that tortured him and simply waited for someone to come and help him.

And there his mother found him. When he saw her he got up immediately, feeling somehow comforted at once, yet humiliated, too, in the very depths of his being, so sure was he of the advice she would give him to proceed upon his chosen way.

But at the first sight of him her worn face grew pale, as though refined through grief.

"Paul!" she cried. "What are you doing there? Are you ill?"

"Mother," he said, walking to the front door without turning into the dining-room, "I did not want to wake you last night, it was so late. Well, I went to see her. I went to see her..."

His mother had already recovered her composure and stood looking fixedly at him. In the brief silence that followed his words they could hear the church bell ringing quickly and insistently as though it were right over the house.

"She is quite well," continued Paul "but she is very excited and insists that I shall leave the place at once: otherwise she threatens to come to church and create a scandal by denouncing me before the congregation."

His mother kept silence, but he felt her at his side, stern and steadfast, upholding him, supporting him as she had supported his earliest steps.

"She wanted me to go away this very night. And she said that... if I did not go, she would come to church this morning... I am not afraid of her: besides, I don't believe she will come."

He opened the front door and a flood of golden light poured into the dark little passage, as though trying to entice him and his mother out into the sunshine. Paul walked towards the church without turning round, and his mother stood at the door looking after him.

She had not opened her lips, but a slight trembling seized her again, and only with an effort could she maintain her outward composure. All at once she went up to her bedroom and hurriedly dressed for church: she was going too, and she, too, drew in her belt and walked with firm steps. And before she left the house she remembered to drive out the intruding chickens again, and to draw the coffee-pot to the side of the fire; then she twisted the long end of her scarf over her mouth and chin to hide the obstinate trembling that would persist in spite of all her efforts to overcome it.

So it was only with a glance of the eyes that she could return the greetings of the women who were coming up from the village, and of the old men already seated on the low parapet round the square before the church, their black pointed caps standing out in sharp relief against the background of rosy morning sky.

Meanwhile Paul had gone into the church.

A few eager penitents were waiting for him, gathered round the confessional; the woman who had arrived first was already kneeling at the little grating, whilst the others waited their turn in the benches close by.

Nina Masia was kneeling on the floor under the holy-water stoup, which looked as though it were resting on her wicked little head, while several boys who were early astir were gathered in a circle round her. Hurrying in with his thoughts elsewhere the priest knocked up against them, and his anger rose instantly as he recognized the girl, who had been placed there by her mother on purpose that she might attract attention. She seemed to be always in his way, at once a hindrance and a reproach.

"Clear out of this instantly!" he bade them, in a voice so loud that it was heard all over the church; and immediately the circle of boys spread itself out and moved a little farther off, with Nina still in the middle, but they grouped themselves round her in such a way that she could be seen by everyone. The women all turned their heads to look at her, though without interrupting their prayers for an instant: she really looked as if she were the idol of the barbaric little church, redolent of the smell of the fields brought in by the peasants and flooded with the rosy haze of a country morning.

Paul walked straight up the nave, but his secret anguish grew ever greater. As he passed, his cassock brushed against the seat where Agnes usually sat; it was the old family pew, the kneeling-stool in front of it richly carved, and with his eyes and measured paces he calculated the distance between it and the altar.

"If I watch for the moment when she rises to carry out her fatal threat I shall have time to get into the sacristy" was his conclusion, and he shivered now as he entered.

Antiochus had hurried down from the belfry to help Paul robe himself, and was waiting for him beside the open cupboard where his vestments hung. He had a pale and serious, almost tragic air, as though already overshadowed by the future career which had been settled for him the previous evening. But the gravity was transient and a smile flickered over the boy's face, just fresh from the wind-swept belfry; his eyes sparkled with joy beneath their decorously lowered lids, and he had to bite his lips to check the ready laugh; his young heart responded to all the radiance, the inspirations, the joyousness of that festal morning. Then his eyes clouded suddenly as he was arranging the lace of the alb over the priest's wrist and he shot a quick look at his master, for he had perceived that the hand beneath the lace was trembling and he saw that the beloved face was pallid and distraught.

"Do you feel ill, sir?"

Paul did feel ill, although he shook his head in denial. He felt as though his mouth were full of blood, yet a tiny germ of hope was springing up in the midst of his distress.

"I shall fall down dead, my heart will break; and then, at least, there will be an end of everything."

He went down into the church again to hear the confessions of the women, and saw his mother at the bottom of the nave near the door. Stern and motionless she knelt there, keeping watch over all who entered the church, over the whole church itself, ready, apparently, to support and hold it up were it even to collapse upon her head.

But he had no more courage left: only that tiny germ of hope within his heart, the hope of death, grew and grew till the breath in him stifled and failed.

When he was seated inside the confessional he felt somewhat calmer; it was like being in a grave, but at least he was hidden from view and could look his horror in the face. The subdued whispering of the women behind the gratings, broken by their little sighs and their warm breath, was like the rustling of lizards in the long grass on the ridge. And Agnes was there too, safe in the secret retreat where he had so often taken her in his thoughts. And the soft breathing of the young women, the scent of their hair and their gala dress, all perfumed with lavender, mingled with his distress and further inflamed his passion.

And he gave them all absolution, absolved them from all their sins, thinking that perhaps before many days had passed he himself would be a suppliant to them for their compassion.

Then he was seized with the craving to get out, to see whether Agnes had arrived. But her seat was empty.

Perhaps she was not coming after all. Yet sometimes she remained at the bottom of the church, kneeling on a chair which her servant brought for her. He turned to look, but saw only his mother's rigid figure, and as he knelt before the altar and began the Mass, he felt that her soul was bending before God, clothed in her grief as he was clothed in his alb and stole.

Then he determined not to look behind him again, to close his eyes each time he had to turn round to give the blessing. He felt as if he were climbing ever higher up some steep and stony Calvary, and a sensation of giddiness seized him whenever the ritual obliged him to face the congregation. Then he closed his eyes to shut out the sight of the abyss that yawned at his feet; but even through his closed eyelids he saw the carven bench and the figure of Agnes, her black dress standing out in relief against the grey wall of the church.

And Agnes was really there, dressed in black with a black veil round her ivory-white face; her eyes were fixed on her prayer-book, the gilt clasp of which glittered in her black-gloved hands, but she never turned a page. The servant with the head of a slave was kneeling on the floor of the aisle beside the bench, and every now and then she raised her eyes, like a faithful dog, to her mistress's face, as though in silent sympathy with the sad thoughts that possessed her.

And he beheld everything from his place at the altar and hope died within him; only from the bottom of his heart he told himself it was impossible that Agnes would carry out her insane threat. He turned the pages of the Gospel, but his faltering voice could scarcely pronounce the words; he broke into a sweat of apprehension, and caught hold of the book as he felt himself fainting.

In a moment he pulled himself together. Antiochus was looking at him, watching the awful change that came over his face as over the face of a corpse, keeping close beside him to support him if he fell, and glancing at the old men by the altar rails to see if they had noticed the priest's distress. But nobody noticed it, even his mother remained in her place, praying and waiting without seeing anything amiss with her son. Then Antiochus drew still closer to him with a protecting movement, so that Paul looked round startled, but the boy gave him a reassuring glance out of his bright eyes, as much as to say: "I am here, it's all right, go on...".

And he went on, climbing that steep Calvary till the blood flowed back into his heart and the tension of his nerves relaxed. But it was the relaxation of despair, the abandonment to danger, the quiet of the drowning man who has no more strength to battle with the waves. When he turned again to the congregation he did not close his eyes.

"The Lord be with you."

Agnes was there in her place, bent over the page she never turned, the gilt clasp of the book shining in the dim light. The servant was crouching at her feet and all the other women, including his mother at the bottom of the church, were sitting back on their heels on the bare floor, ready to resume their kneeling position immediately the priest should move the book.

And he moved the book and went on with the prayers and the slow gestures of the ritual. And a feeling of tenderness crept into his despair at the thought that Agnes was bearing him company on his road to Calvary, as Mary had followed too, that in another moment she would mount the altar steps and stand beside him once again, having overcome their transgression, to expiate together as together they had sinned. How could he hate her if she brought his punishment with her, if her hatred was only love disguised?

Then came the Communion, and the few drops of wine went down into his breast like quickening blood; he felt strong, revived, his heart filled with the presence of God.

And as he descended the steps towards the women the figure of Agnes in her seat stood out prominent amidst the crowd of bowed heads. She, too, had bowed her head upon her hands; perhaps she was summoning her courage before she moved. And suddenly he felt infinite pity for her; he would have liked to go down to her and give her absolution, and administer the Communion as to a dying woman. He, too, had summoned his courage, but his hands shook as he held the wafer to the women's lips.

Immediately the Communion was ended an old peasant began to intone a hymn. The congregation sang the verses after him in subdued voices, and repeated the antiphons twice out loud. The hymn was primitive and monotonous, old as the earliest prayers of man uttered in forests where as yet scarcely man dwelt, old and monotonous as the breaking of waves on a solitary shore; yet that low singing around her sufficed to bring Agnes's thoughts back, as though she had been rushing breathless by night through some primeval forest and had suddenly emerged upon the seashore, amidst sandhills covered with sweet flowers and golden in the light of dawn.

Something stirred in the very depths of her being, a strange emotion gripped her throat; she felt the world turning round with her as though she had been walking head downwards and now resumed her natural position.

It was her past and the past of all her race that surged up and took hold of her, with the singing of the women and the old men, with the voices of her nurse and her servants, the men and women who had built and furnished her house, and ploughed her fields and woven the linen for her swaddling clothes.

How could she denounce herself before all these people who looked up to her as their mistress and held her even purer than the priest at the altar? And then she, too, felt the presence of God around her and within her, even in her passion itself.

She knew very well that the punishment she meant to inflict upon the man with whom she had sinned was her own punishment too; but now a merciful God spoke to her with the voices of the old men and women and the innocent children, and bade her beware of her own self, counselled her to seek salvation.

As her people round her sang the verses of the hymn, all the days of her solitary life unrolled themselves before her inward vision. She saw herself again a little child, then a young girl, then a grown woman in this same church, on this same seat blackened and worn by the elbows and knees of her forefathers. In a sense the church belonged to her family; it had been built by one of her ancestors, and tradition said that the image of the Madonna had been captured from Barbary pirates and brought back to the village by a far-away grandfather of hers.

She had been born and brought up amidst these traditions, in an atmosphere of simple grandeur that kept her aloof from the smaller people of Aar, yet still in the midst of them, shut in amongst them like a pearl in its rough shell.

How could she denounce herself before her people? But this very feeling of being mistress even of the sacred building rendered more insufferable still the presence of the man who had been her companion in sin, and who appeared at the altar wearing a mask of saintliness and bearing the holy vessels in his hands. Tall and splendid he stood above her as she knelt at his feet, guilty in that she had loved him.

Her heart swelled anew with rage and grief as the hymn rose and fell around her, like a supplication rising from out some abyss, imploring help and justice, and she heard the voice of God, dark and stern, bidding her drive His unworthy servant out of His temple.

She grew pale as death and broke into a cold sweat; her knees shook against the seat, but she bowed no more and with head erect she watched the movements of the priest at the altar. And it was as though some evil breath went out from her to him, paralysing him, enveloping him in the same icy grip that held her fast.

And he felt that mortal breath that emanated from her will, and just as on bitter winter mornings, his fingers were frozen and uncontrollable shivers ran down his spine. When he turned to give the benediction he saw Agnes gazing at him. Their eyes met as in a flash, and like a drowning man he remembered in that instant all the joy of his life, joy sprung wholly and solely from love of her, from the first look of her eyes, the first kiss of her lips.

Then he saw her rise from her seat, book in hand.

"Oh God, Thy will be done" he stammered, kneeling – he seemed to be actually in the Garden of Olives – and watching the shadow of an inexorable fate.

He prayed aloud and waited, and midst the confused sound of the people's prayers he thought he could distinguish Agnes's step as she moved toward the altar.

"She is coming... she has left her seat, she is between her seat and the altar. She is coming... she is here... everyone is staring at her. She is at my side!"

The obsession was so strong that the words failed on his lips. He saw Antiochus, who had already begun to extinguish the candles, suddenly turn and look round, and he knew for certain that she was there, close to him, on the chancel steps.

He rose to his feet, the roof seemed to fall down upon his head and fracture it; his knees scarcely upheld him, but with a sudden effort he managed to get up to the altar again and take the pyx. And as he turned to enter the sacristy he saw that Agnes had advanced from her seat to the railing and was about to mount the steps.

"Oh, Lord, why not let me die?" and he bowed his head over the pyx as though baring his neck to the sword that was about to strike it. But as he entered the sacristy door he looked again and perceived Agnes bowed at the altar railing as she knelt on the lowest step.

She had stumbled at the lowest step outside the railing, and as though a wall had suddenly risen up before her, she had dropped on her knees. A thick mist dimmed her sight and she could go no further.

Presently the dimness cleared and she could see the steps again, the yellow carpet before the altar, the flowers upon the table and the burning lamp. But the priest had disappeared, and in his place a ray of sunlight smote obliquely through the dusk and made a golden patch upon the carpet.

She crossed herself, rose to her feet and moved towards the door. The servant followed her and the old men, the women and the children turned to smile at her and bless her with their eyes; she was their mistress, their symbol of beauty and of faith, so far removed from them and yet in the midst of them and all their misery, like a wild rose amongst the brambles.

At the church door the servant offered her holy water on the tips of her fingers, and then stooped to brush off the dust of the altar steps which still clung to her dress. As the girl raised herself again she saw the ashen face of Agnes turned towards the corner where the priest's mother had knelt through all the service. Then she saw the mother sitting motionless on the ground, her head sunk forward on her breast, her shoulders leaning against the wall as though she had made a supreme effort to uphold *it* in a great collapse. Noticing the fixed gaze of Agnes and the servant, a woman also turned to look, then sprang quickly to the side of the priest's mother, spoke to her in a whisper and raised her face in her hand.

The mother's eyes were half-closed, glassy, the pupils up-turned; the rosary had dropped from her hand and her head fell sideways on to the shoulder of the woman who held her.

"She is dead!" shrieked the woman.

And instantly the whole congregation was on its feet and crowding to the bottom of the church.

Meanwhile Paul had gone back into the sacristy with Antiochus, who was carrying the book of the Gospel. He was trembling with cold and with relief; he actually felt as though he had just escaped from a shipwreck, and he wanted to energize and walk about to warm himself and convince himself that it had all been a bad dream.

Then a confused murmur of voices was heard in the church, at first low, then growing quickly louder and louder. Antiochus put his head out of the sacristy door and saw all the people collected together at the bottom of the nave, as though there were some obstruction at the entrance, but an old man was already hastening up the chancel steps and making mysterious signs.

"His mother is taken ill" he said.

Paul, still robed in his alb, was down there at one bound and threw himself on his knees that he might look more closely into his mother's face as she lay stretched on the ground, with her head in a woman's lap and hemmed in by the pressing crowd.

"Mother, mother!"

The face was still and rigid, the eyes half-closed, the teeth clenched in the effort not to cry aloud.

And he knew instantly that she had died of the shock of that same grief, that same terror which he had been enabled to overcome.

And he, too, clenched his teeth that he might not cry aloud when he raised his head; and across the confused mass of the people surging round, his eyes met the eyes of Agnes fixed upon him.

CHARACTER NAMES

All the names of the main and minor characters of the short novel *La madre* (The Mother) have a biblical or religious origin. The arrangement is so striking and the reputation of the Author is such that coincidence as an explanation is most unlikely. References to the Old and New Testament are spread throughout the story. It is seemingly possible that Grazia Deledda loved playing with names, since most of the characters of the novel are in antithesis with their historical counterparts.

PAUL: the priest in love with Agnes. Paul is the name taken later in life by Saul of Tarsus, commonly known as Saint Paul. After his conversion "on the road to Damascus", he who was a prosecutor of Christians became one of the most devoted Apostles of Christ. Even though he never personally met Jesus, he is considered the most important preacher of the first generation of Christians. Thirteen of the 27 books of the New Testament are attributed to him. He was strongly convinced that celibacy had to be practised by the followers of Christ.

AGNES: the woman in love with Paul. Saint Agnes of Rome (c. 291 – c. 304 AD) is venerated as a Virgin Martyr. She is the patron saint of Chastity and Virgins and is usually depicted with a lamb.

MARIA MADDALENA: the mother of the priest. The name directly refers to Mary Magdalene of the New Testament. According to the four official Gospels, she was the most devoted follower of Christ and assisted at his crucifixion, burial and resurrection. According to other sources she was the companion of Jesus of Nazareth.

ANTIOCHUS: the altar boy who wants to become a priest. In Jewish history, Antiochus IV *Epiphanes* 'God manifest' (c. 215 – 164 BC) king of the Seleucid Empire – also called Antiochus *Epimanes* 'the madman' – is considered a major villain. He outlawed Jewish rites and traditions in his attempt to completely Hellenize their culture and this was probably one of the major causes of the

Maccabean revolt. Some scholars argue that his rule was foreseen in the Book of Daniel and that he is also a foreshadowing of the coming Antichrist. Saint Antiochus of Sulcis (died c. 110 AD) is the first martyr saint of Sardinia and one of the most venerated in the island; a small island and a town are named after him.

NICODEMUS PANIA (nicknamed King Nicodemus in the novel): an almost pagan hunter who lives in a hut up in the mountains, much respected in the village. He is dying, so Paul is summoned for the last rites and the extreme unction. In the Gospel of John, Nicodemus is described as a Pharisee who came to talk to Jesus "at night" and also as a leader of the Jews (ambiguous personality). He assisted Joseph of Arimathea during the burial of Jesus. The Gospel of Nicodemus is an apocryphal work which bears his name. *Pania* is an Italian word meaning 'birdlime', "*liberarsi dalla pania*" means 'to free oneself from a bond or an embarrassing situation'. Nicodemus is not a common name and Grazia Deledda must have used it for a precise reason. In his conversation with Jesus, Nicodemus asks the meaning of "to be born again". During the Protestant-Catholic struggle in Europe, from the 16th to the 18th Century, the term *Nicodemite* was developed to indicate a person who was suspected of false public exhibition of their actual religious beliefs. In the novel, Paul spends a significant portion of the two and a half days in which the plot develops by following him to his mountain refuge. And this while he has pressing problems back at home, but when he returns he is not a man "born again" but still the ambiguous man he used to be.

NINA MASIA: the girl exorcised by Paul. Nina is the short version of the name *Annina* which is the diminutive of the biblical name *Hannah* 'favour, grace'. In the New Testament it is the name of a prophetess who recognised Jesus as the Messiah. The word *masia* – which may be assonated to *messiah* – in Sardinian means 'country dwelling' (of Catalan origin).

MARIELENA: a woman in the story who cuddles Paul as a boy and «perhaps she had been his first love»; it is from her garden that young Paul and Maria Paska (see below) look steadily at each other for the first time. The name is the combination of Mary and Helen of Greek origin 'shining light, moon'. Saint Helena Empress is the mother of Emperor Costantine the Great. She is an important figure in the history of Christianity because of her influence on her son and because she allegedly found the "True Cross" during a tour in Palestine.

MARIA PASKA: the «lost woman» Paul engages with before taking his vows. The name Mary is of uncertain origin, probably ancient Egyptian meaning 'loved by God', but she is best known as the mother of Jesus. Paska comes from the latin word *pascha* which is a derivation of the Hebrew *pesah* 'pass over, go beyond'. Jews celebrate Passover to commemorate the Exodus while Christians celebrate Easter (*Pasqua* in Italian) to honour the resurrection of Jesus Christ.

MARCO PANIZZA (mentioned only once): a devoted parishioner of Aar. Mark is one of the four Evangelists and a follower of St. Paul. *Panizza* in Italian is a polenta made with chickpea flour. The word could also be derived from *panizu* which in Sardinian means 'nickname'.

ILARIO PANIZZA: the son of the devoted parishioner, possible antagonist of Antiochus as altar boy. This is the only name which does not have a biblical origin. Ilario derives from the Greek *hilaros* meaning 'cheerful, joyous, prompt to do anything'. Pope Saint Hilarius was the first pope born in Sardinia (died in Rome, 468 AD).

AAR: in the novel, a poor remote hillside village in Sardinia. According to historical records, no place in the island – town or locality – bears or ever had such a name. No word in Sardinian starts with or even contains a double 'a'. It could however be considered a diminutive of the Greek form *Aaron* derived from the Hebrew *Aharon*, mentioned in the Bible as the elder brother of Moses, a prophet and the first High Priest of the Israelites: therefore *Aar* > town of the High Priest. According to other theories, the name could be derived from various Hebrew roots meaning 'high mountain, mountain of strength'.

F.C.

The Author

GRAZIA MARIA COSIMA DAMIANA DELEDDA (Nuoro, 28th September 1871 – Rome, 15th August 1936) was an Italian writer who received the Nobel Prize for Literature for 1926 on 10th December 1927 «for her idealistically inspired writings which with plastic clarity picture the life on her native island and with depth and sympathy deal with human problems in general». She was the first, and so far, only Italian woman writer to receive this honour.

Born into a middle-class family, she attended Primary school and then was educated by a private tutor. She started writing at a young age and kept reading and studying literature on her own. Her career began by publishing short stories in the fashion magazine *L'ultima moda* but her family did not encourage her desire to write. In 1900 Deledda marries Palmiro Madesani and moves to Rome, where she lived for the rest of her life.

Her first novel, published in 1888 at the age of 17, was *Memorie di Fernanda*. A collection of short stories, *Nell'azzurro*, followed in 1890. She then went on to write over thirty-five novels and about four hundred short stories. Among her most important works are: *Elias Portolu* (1900), the story of a mystical former convict in love with his brother's bride; *Dopo il divorzio* (1902; *After the Divorce*); *Cenere* (1903; *Ashes*), in which an illegitimate son causes his mother's suicide; *L'edera* (1908); *Canne al vento* (1913; *Reeds in the Wind*); *Marianna Sirca* (1915); *L'incendio nell'oliveto* (1918); *La madre* (1920; *The Woman and the Priest*, U.S. title, *The Mother*) which is considered to be the novel that won her the Nobel Prize. Her later works include: *Il segreto dell'uomo solitario* (1921), *Il Dio dei viventi* (1922), *La fuga in Egitto* (1925), *Annalena Bilsini* (1927), *Il paese del vento* (1931). Her last work, *Cosima* (published posthumously in 1936) is her most autobiographical.

Her writing seems to focus on portraying harsh realities, combining imagination and autobiographical elements. Her novels tend to criticize social values and moral norms rather than the people who are victims of such circumstances. Most of Deledda's works are based on strong facts of love, pain and death upon which rests the inevitable sensation of sin and doom. Within Deledda's novels there is always a strong connection between places and people, feelings and environment. In the background of most of her stories we find the life, customs, and traditions of her homeland, Sardinia.

She died in Rome at the age of 64 and now rests at the *Chiesa della Solitudine* in Nuoro.

Titles in the series "Le Grazie", by Grazia Deledda

Memorie di Fernanda, 1888
Nell'azzurro, 1890
Stella d'oriente, 1890
Fior di Sardegna, 1891
Racconti sardi, 1894
Tradizioni popolari di Nuoro in Sardegna, 1894
Anime oneste, 1895 (*Honest Souls*, 2009)[1]
La via del male, 1896
L'ospite, 1897
Il tesoro, 1897
Le tentazioni, 1899
La giustizia, 1899
Il vecchio della montagna, 1899
Elias Portolu, 1900 (*Elias Portolu*, 1992)
La regina delle tenebre, 1901
Dopo il divorzio, 1902 – **After the Divorce**, 1905
Cenere, 1903 (*Ashes*, 2004)
Nostalgie, 1905
I giuochi della vita, 1905
Amori moderni, 1907
L'ombra del passato, 1907
Il nonno, 1908
L'edera, 1908
Il nostro padrone, 1910
Sino al confine, 1910
Nel deserto, 1911
Chiaroscuro, 1912 (*"Chiaroscuro" and Other Stories*, 2004)
Colombi e sparvieri, 1912
Canne al vento, 1913 (*Reeds in the Wind*, 1999)
Le colpe altrui, 1914
Il fanciullo nascosto, 1915

----

1) Within brackets are reported the available English translations which are not part of this series.

Marianna Sirca, 1915 (*Marianna Sirca*, 2006)
L'incendio nell'oliveto, 1917-1918
Il ritorno del figlio, 1919
La madre, 1919 – **The Mother** (*The Woman and the Priest*), 1922
Il segreto dell'uomo solitario, 1921
Il Dio dei viventi, 1922
Il flauto nel bosco, 1923
La danza della collana, 1924
La fuga in Egitto, 1925
Il sigillo d'amore, 1926
Annalena Bilsini, 1927
Il vecchio e i fanciulli, 1928
Il dono di Natale, 1930
La casa del poeta, 1930
Il paese del vento, 1931
La vigna sul mare, 1932
Sole d'estate, 1933
L'argine, 1934
La chiesa della solitudine, 1936 (*The Church of Solitude*, 2002)
Cosima, 1936 (*Cosima*, 1988)

All titles are available in ebook format (epub, Kindle).

Made in the USA
Columbia, SC
05 August 2021

43026955R00074